Myrna Mackenzie grew up not having a clue what she wanted to be—she hadn't been born a princess, the one job she thought she might like because of the steady flow of pretty dresses and crowns—but she knew that she loved stories and happy endings, so falling into life as a romance writer was pretty much inevitable. An award-winning author, with over 35 novels written, Myrna was born in a small town in Dunklin County, Missouri, grew up just outside Chicago, and now divides her time between two lakes in Chicago and Wisconsi—both very different and both very beautiful. She adores the internet (which still seems magical after all these years), loves coffee, hiking, attempting gardening (without much success), cooking and knitting.

Readers (and other potential gardeners, cooks, knitters, writers, etc.) can visit Myrna online at www.myrnamackenzie.com, or write to her at PO Box 225, La Grange, IL 60525, USA.

"That's it! That's the last time I trust so blindly. Ever," Rachel muttered out loud as the sound of the car died away. For long seconds she couldn't even think about what to do or where to go in this unfamiliar town. She simply stood in the middle of the street alone.

Or...not alone. A sound across the street made the breath catch in her throat. Immediately her senses went on high alert. She opened her eyes...and locked gazes with a tall, broad-shouldered man who, by the way he was looking at her, had clearly witnessed the whole exchange. Some sort of cowboy type, judging by his boots, his jeans and his bronzed skin. He was standing just outside a store and must have been on the verge of entering or leaving when she and Dennis had begun their little scene. Her most personal failings had been viewed by this stranger.

She glared at him.

He didn't look even remotely fazed. "Do you need help?" he asked, in a deep, whisky-rough voice that sounded as if it came straight from some rugged cowboy movie.

Did she need help?

Yes—oh, yes, she thought, as a sense of loss and failure tugged at her heart.

"No, thank you," she said primly, willing him to walk away so that she could figure out her next step in private. She tried to smile more broadly, lifting her chin and practically daring him to repudiate her words.

TO WED
A RANCHER

BY
MYRNA MACKENZIE

MILLS & BOON

First published in Great Britain 2011
by Mills & Boon, an imprint of Harlequin (UK) Limited,
Eton House, 18-24 Paradise Road, Richmond, Surrey TW9 1SR

© Myrna Topol 2011

ISBN: 978 0 263 22085 8

Harlequ|
and rec|
forests.
legal er

Printec
by CPI Antony Rowe, Chippenham, Wiltshire

CHAPTER ONE

"I'm sorry. It's obvious that I made a mistake. I was wrong to trust you. So, please, just go." Rachel Everly's voice wasn't as steady as she wanted it to be, but she managed to turn away from the car and the man she'd thought she'd known up until a few days ago.

"Rachel, stop acting stupid and hysterical. You're totally overreacting, so just get back in the car and let's go. Besides, I'm still your boss until this trip is over, and we have a photo shoot in Oregon in two days."

Oh, no, had Dennis really used the S word? And called her hysterical? *And* implied that trying to make another woman jealous by lying and saying he and Rachel were sleeping together was okay when he had claimed to have hired Rachel for her skill with a camera?

This morning, listening to him talking to the woman and then having him admit that his lies about Rachel had his ex-girlfriend wild to have him back, reality had hit Rachel hard. Dennis had been lying to her all along. He wasn't her friend. He wasn't fascinated by her skill as a photographer. He was a jerk who was just using her. And she had been used before.

No more.

Rachel wanted to whirl back toward the car and tell

him what she thought, but right now she was almost as angry at herself as she was with him. Darn it, she *had* acted stupidly. She'd always prided herself on being nobody's fool, but the man had discovered her weakness. He'd used their shared interest in photography to make her feel unique, when she was clearly just a convenience who could serve both as an assistant and a lure to play another woman for a fool. Using photography, her greatest passion, against her was…not cool. But allowing herself to be used was even worse. She needed to get out of here with as much dignity as she could muster.

She pushed her shoulders back. "You'll have to find a new assistant for Oregon. You're not my boss anymore. I'm through with you." With that, she walked away.

Behind her, there was silence. Then Dennis let loose with a string of profanities, his tires squealing as he drove away. She closed her eyes.

"That's it, Everly! That's the last time I trust so blindly. Ever," she muttered out loud as the sound of the car died away. For long seconds she couldn't even think about what to do or where to go in this unfamiliar town. She simply stood in the middle of the street alone.

Or…not alone. The sound of something scuffling against the pavement made her breath catch in her throat. Immediately her senses went on high alert. She opened her eyes…and locked gazes with a tall, broad-shouldered man who, by the way he was looking at her, had clearly witnessed the whole exchange. Some sort of cowboy type judging by his boots, his jeans and his bronzed skin. He was standing just outside a store and must have been on the verge of entering or leaving when she and Dennis had begun their little scene. Her most personal failings had been viewed by this stranger.

She glared at him.

He didn't look even remotely fazed. "Do you need help?" he asked in a deep, whiskey-rough voice that sounded as if it came straight from some rugged cowboy movie.

Did she need help?

Yes, she thought, as a sense of failure tugged at her heart. Her past hadn't been the type that led her to build relationships. And, while this hadn't been a longstanding relationship, she'd thought she and Dennis had had something in common. She'd been wrong. Even worse, she'd been weak, and consequently blind.

Now, because of that uncharacteristic blindness, here she was. Alone. She was...she didn't even know where she was. Somewhere with a lot of cows and boots and cowboy stuff. In Montana. And talking to a stranger who had witnessed her humiliation. Still, she should be grateful for his offer, and a part of her was, but mostly she just wanted to escape those tooperceptive silver-blue eyes.

"I...what town is this?"

"Moraine. Do you need a lift somewhere?"

Oh, yeah, like she was going to get in a car with a stranger. She might have made a rookie mistake where Dennis was concerned, but she'd grown up around some big, bad cities. She'd taken her share of self-defense classes and knew how to behave when approached by unfamiliar men.

"No, thank you," she said primly. "I'm perfectly fine. I know exactly where I'm going and how to get there. I have friends." Which was, of course, a total lie.

But, self-defense classes or not, the thought of letting a man so much taller and more muscular than she was know that she was totally on her own in the middle of all this emptiness…if he carted her off somewhere, no one would ever even know she was gone.

"I have plans," she said more firmly, willing him to walk away so that she could figure out her next step in private. She tried to smile more broadly, lifting her chin and practically daring him to repudiate her words.

He studied her for several seconds, frowning all the while. Then he nodded once, turning away. Somehow, despite what she'd told him, a totally unreasonable part of her resented just how quickly he'd moved on. Maybe because men were not on her *nice* list right now. Especially tall, good-looking men. And, unfortunately, *this* tall man was gorgeous. He probably had women sending him sexy messages every half-hour. Irrational as it might be, it was easy to transfer her anger to him.

And then things got worse. When the man moved closer to the door of the store and turned slightly, looking back at her, she was sure she saw pity in his eyes.

A groan nearly escaped her. Pity was the worst. Maybe because she'd been forced to choke it down too many times in the past. She narrowed her eyes and pulled herself up to her full five foot three inches. "Did you need something?" she asked, trying to make it look as if she was the one in charge of her life and he was the one who merited sympathy.

He stared at her. She stared right back, doing her best to look totally unaffected by the recent turn of events.

"Not a thing," he said as he gave her one last dismissive look and walked away.

Immediately Rachel's anger vanished. No question

she was acting ungrateful and being unfair. But then, this whole situation was unfair.

Still, self-pity got a person nowhere, and she was used to depending on herself. So she turned and marched away as if she had a true destination in mind, when in fact she hadn't a clue.

It was only after she'd turned the corner and realized that she was already almost on the edge of town, with nothing beyond but lots of big, yawning stretches of land, that she began to panic.

"Stop, Rachel. Slow down. Think," she ordered herself, echoing the words of a favorite teacher. *What are the facts? What's the situation? What's the logical next step?* Good questions for an impulsive person like herself.

Questions she hadn't asked herself when she'd gotten out of the car. The truth was that she had been so shocked when the message and accompanying photo of that scantily dressed woman had appeared on the screen of Dennis's phone that she had simply reacted. The realization that she had been manipulated and used to con and hurt another woman had made her sick.

But now here she was, with no job and nowhere to go. Having planned to work with Dennis on the west coast, she'd given up her apartment. Her mother was on her umpteenth honeymoon, and her father's new wife felt about Rachel the way most people felt about gum on their shoes. And…

"My phone and my wallet were in the glove compartment of Dennis's car," she realized with a horrified whisper. It was enough to make some women sit down in the middle of the road and cry.

Rachel tried not to be that kind of woman most of

the time. *There's an upside to most situations,* she reminded herself. Unfortunately she was having trouble finding the upside right now, and time was against her. A few hours from now it would be dark. She'd need a place to sleep…and some way to pay for it.

Battling panic, she veered back toward the town. She glanced down at her camera, her one constant companion, the one thing she had always been able to depend on. Still, it wouldn't help her today.

She headed toward a small building with the words "Angie's Diner" on the window. There was only one customer and a large, friendly-looking woman behind the counter. Rachel opened the door and the bell jangled. The woman looked up and smiled.

"Can I help you?"

Rachel wanted to close her eyes at the prospect of begging for work. Instead, she took a deep breath and managed to paste on a smile. "Hi, I'm Rachel Everly. Are you Angie?"

"None other."

"Nice to meet you. Is there any chance that you're hiring?"

Angie looked around the almost empty room. The clock seemed to tick too loudly, emphasizing the lack of customers. "Sorry, no. You're new in town." It wasn't even a question. This was obviously one of those places where everyone knew everyone.

"I'm…visiting." Rachel didn't try to explain why she would need work if she wasn't staying. "Is there any place to stay in town?"

"Just Ruby's boarding house. Good food and service with a smile." Angie fired off directions. "But if you want work…well, good luck. Not much around here."

Rachel tried to tamp down her anxiety. "Thank

you." She wandered back into the street. Maybe if she humbled herself and begged, or offered to help Ruby with dishes or something, she could at least get through the night. Tomorrow she would figure out the next step, but she knew one thing. She was going to be extremely wary of men and their motives from now on. Because of idiotically trusting Dennis, she was homeless, stranded in the middle of nowhere.

"That's temporary," she told herself, battling her fears. Someday she'd finally have the home she'd never had. In Maine, the one place she'd been happy and the place she'd been trying to get back to for a long time. She'd be there now if...

Stop thinking about your mistakes. That isn't helping. Right now she had to concentrate on finding a bed. Maybe she could barter a free advertising photo of the boarding house for a place to stay, reach some sort of deal.

Just thinking the words made her feel a bit better. At least she wouldn't have to deal with any more men today. Her experience with the cowboy in town had been...well, she wasn't going to think about that. She'd never see the man again, anyway.

Shane Merritt wasn't in the best of moods. Being back in Montana, even temporarily, had him edgy, and that encounter with the woman in town hadn't done a thing for his bad mood. He hated feeling responsible for other people. He had a past that proved he was the worst kind of guy to turn to for help, but it had been clear from the little he'd seen that she was stranded in Moraine. It had also been clear that she didn't want his assistance.

"Which you ought to be grateful for, Merritt. The

woman did you a massive favor when she turned you down." The truth was that he was itching to get back on the road, back to his wandering life and his business that allowed him to keep moving. But he couldn't do that yet. He was as stuck here as she was, so for now he was going to have to settle for getting these supplies back to the ranch.

Unfortunately, his cell phone rang at that moment. "What's up, Jim?" Shane asked his business manager.

"Trouble. Your next job needs a reschedule. There's a conflict and you need to be in Germany in two weeks."

Shane blew out a breath. "Jim, you know I'm held up here until I sell the ranch. When I got here…well, let's just say that Oak Valley is in worse condition than I thought. Try to buy me at least three weeks." Even though in some ways the shorter time frame would be less draining. He'd inherited the family ranch a year ago, and for months he'd been eager to sell his less than happy childhood home, but this was the first time he'd had time to fly in and get the job done properly. And he needed to do it himself. There were things here…things that had belonged to his mother and his brother…

The overwhelming pain that followed that thought served as a reminder that he had failed them, and that, difficult as it was, he needed to be the one to supervise the disposal of their personal effects.

That conviction increased his resolve. "See what you can do, but three weeks is the absolute minimum for me to put things to rights. Things here look pretty messed up." Which was his own fault for staying away and letting things deteriorate.

"You okay?" his friend and employee asked.

No. Being here brought back memories he had to keep batting away, but at least once this was done it would be over, or as over as it would ever get. He never had to come back here again. He could spend the rest of his life circling the globe a free man. No ties.

"Shane?" Jim's voice was concerned.

"I'm doing just fine," Shane lied. "It's just a bit of an adjustment being back on a ranch after years of living in offices and hotels." That was one way of putting it. The trip to town had been a mistake. Moraine was filled with too many memories, regrets and ghosts. He wouldn't be going back.

"I can hardly picture you on a ranch," Jim was saying. "Or riding a horse or dating a cowgirl. *Are* there any cute cowgirls in the area?"

Immediately the image of the woman in town came to mind. She'd been tiny, pretty, spitting mad and full of grit. And not a cowgirl.

"I wouldn't know. I didn't come here looking for women."

"Yes, but they tend to find you." Jim didn't sound even vaguely concerned that he had wandered into personal territory. They'd known each other a long time. "Sometimes they even follow you here."

"That only happened a couple of times. It's not happening again."

"Too bad. I get some of my best dates that way."

Which was a lie. Jim had women lined up around the block, but Shane appreciated his friend's attempt at levity. It reminded him that there was more to life than selling the ranch. Oak Valley might have colored his world with bitterness at one time, but today it was only a temporary detour in his life. "Make the call to

Germany, Jim. I'll be back in three even if I have to give the place away."

"Will do, but if you meet any cute cowgirls give them my number. I've never been on a ranch." It was a direct bid for an invitation, but Shane didn't fall in line. Oak Valley had never been a place where fun lived. He ended the conversation and headed down the road.

But Jim's comments about women stuck in his mind. Or at least the image of the woman in town did. The scene with her and the man had been tense, the proverbial car wreck a person couldn't look away from. Her chocolate-brown eyes had been vulnerable, but she'd also been defiant and proud. When Shane had dared to suggest that she might need help she'd given him a withering look, as if she was offended...or suspected that he might grow fangs and fur every full moon.

So he'd backed off, which was a good thing. Despite those eyes that made a man think of dark nights and pleasure, the last thing he needed was to get even remotely involved with a woman he associated with Moraine, especially one with trust issues.

Besides, right now his life was centered on work and on expanding his business into more distant markets. It was a good life. It was enough.

"So, back to business, Merritt." The clock was ticking away, even faster now that he knew he had only three weeks. But this darn task...like it or not, he needed at least a little help. Some extra muscle, a short-term housekeeper and cook, someone who could take photos to help with the sales package.

"Hell." The word slipped out as he glanced up ahead and saw a small figure trudging down the gravel road, a red duffle bag banging against one leg, a very expensive Hasselblad he hadn't noticed before hugged tight against her other side. Her legs were covered in dust. She already looked beat up. And it was miles to anywhere.

He swore again beneath his breath, then pulled up beside her, prepared for another round of *Get away from me. I don't need any help.* He wanted to keep moving like fire wanted fuel, but several things stopped him. She was alone on a lonely road with night drawing near, and he couldn't just leave her alone in the dark. The woman didn't even have a flashlight to guide her; she wasn't wearing anything reflective. Besides, he couldn't forget those pretty, distressed eyes...or help wondering whether she could cook and just how skilled she was with that camera....

Rachel heard a car coming up behind her and instinctively stepped farther off the road, hugging her camera closer to her body. Out here in the middle of what had to be Big Sky country, if the ceiling of pure blue was to be trusted, she felt naked, vulnerable. There was absolutely nowhere to go if she needed to run.

Not that she would need it, but self-protection was simply an instinct for someone like her. She took one more step to the right.

The car slowed.

Her heartbeat picked up. She didn't speed up—what was the point?—but she tried to take another step farther away.

"Don't," that deep, already familiar voice ordered as the car stopped. "Barbed wire is very unforgiving."

She stopped dead in her tracks and looked to the right. Okay, there it was. Barbed wire.

"What do you want?" She tried to make her voice

brave as he got out of the car. What would she do if he moved closer?

To her relief, he didn't take another step. He stayed on the driver's side, two tons of metal between them.

"What do I want? Not what you apparently think."

"What do you think I think?" She forced herself to stare him dead in the eyes. Those silver-blue eyes that made her want to look away…or keep staring at him. She frowned.

He scowled down at her thin-soled shoes that hadn't been made for walking long distances. "You're miles from anywhere, you know."

"Is that a threat?" She hoped she sounded brave.

"Not a threat. A fact." He held out his hands, open-palmed, as if to show her that he was weaponless or helpless or…something harmless…which she was sure wasn't true. He was a big man and, even if he wasn't a threat physically, he had that solid heartbreaker look about him. The kind of look that made a woman's chest grow tight and her breathing uneven. She hated that, and, given her recent circumstances and decisions, she looked at him more critically and came to the conclusion that a man like that was not to be trusted. Maybe if she'd done more critical thinking the day Dennis had given a workshop at the camera shop where she'd been working she wouldn't be in this fix now.

"Mind if I ask where you're headed?" he asked.

She did mind. She didn't want to talk to him. But the truth was that she'd been wondering for the past twenty minutes if she was walking in the right direction.

"The woman who runs the diner told me that someone named Ruby would rent me a room."

"She's still doing that, is she?"

Rachel blinked. "Don't you know?"

"I don't live here anymore. But if you're looking for Ruby, then you missed the turn out of town maybe a mile and a half back."

The shot of energy that had run through her earlier had worn off after she'd realized that for now she was lost and stuck, tired and hungry, and in a really bad place. Now, with this bit of bad news, Rachel felt her spirits fall even lower than they already were. "And how far past the turn is her place?"

"Two miles or so."

She forced herself not to sit down in the dirt right then. Instead, she held herself as erect as she could and started to turn around.

"Do you have a phone?" he asked.

"Yes."

"Where is it?"

She didn't want to say. "Why?"

"I'm going to have you call Ruby."

"Does she have a shuttle service?"

The briefest of smiles transformed his handsome face into something truly, outrageously gorgeous before it disappeared as if it had never existed. Rachel wished that she hadn't noticed his looks. They were completely irrelevant and acknowledging them was… not helpful. Not helpful at all.

"A shuttle service? Not that I know of. But if you call her you can ask her about me, so that I can give you a ride."

"Why would you do that?"

"Let's just say that I don't need you on my con-science."

Ordinarily, Rachel would have bristled at that, but right now she was too tired. "How do I know that you and Ruby aren't in cahoots?"

"You don't, but if that's the case then Angie would have to be in with us, too, right?"

He had a point. Rachel wished that her mind wasn't so fried. Getting in a car with a stranger? A handsome, dangerous stranger who was probably used to getting his way simply by offering up a few dimpled smiles? "I'm sorry. I'm from the city. I don't take rides from people I don't know well."

The man blew out a breath. He gave her a look, and what she read in it was probably not what he was really thinking. She had been riding around the country with Dennis, and she clearly didn't know as much about him as she'd thought she had. Still...

"My phone was in the glove compartment of Dennis's car," she admitted.

"I see." He pulled an expensive phone from his pocket and moved just close enough to hand it to her. "I'd give you the number, but I haven't been here for a while."

She nodded, then dialed directory assistance. "What's your name?" she whispered loudly as she dialed Ruby's Rooftop Restaurant and Rooming House.

"Shane Merritt."

"So...Ruby will tell me you're a good guy?"

"No. She'll probably tell you some personal stuff I don't want to think about and that I'm a jackass, but I'm not the kind of jackass who kidnaps women."

Rachel stopped dialing. She stared up at him. "So... even though you've just admitted that you're not a good guy, you just want to give me a ride? That's all this is about?"

"Not exactly. I told you. I'm not stellar material. I do have ulterior motives, but nothing that should make you worry or run in the opposite direction. I have a few simple questions and I need simple answers."

What was this about? A sense of unease settled into her stomach. But this man apparently knew the woman who might, if she was lucky, let her stay the night for free. It wouldn't do to tick him off. "Ask."

He stared directly into her eyes. "How much do you know about cooking and cleaning?"

That was an easy one. Almost nothing. But clearly that would be the wrong answer. That kind of a question sounded as if there was a job attached. Right now, given her dire circumstances, she was entertaining all possibilities. She could always run if she didn't like the questions that followed.

"I know enough," she said carefully, desperately telling herself that it wasn't a lie. *Enough* was a relative answer.

He nodded, but she could tell that wasn't exactly the answer he was seeking. "How well do you know how to use that camera and…is it possible that you have a few weeks to kill?"

As if he'd said something about her child, she wrapped one palm protectively around the Hasselblad. "Okay, now you're creeping me out." She started punching in the numbers for Ruby's place again, as if just hearing a woman's voice would save her from this crazy man. "I don't know what this is about, but I don't take kinky pictures and I can't imagine what you would want with my camera or me or—"

He scowled and held up his hand, those dangerous blue eyes looking even more dangerous. "You're mistaken if you think I'm interested in anything kinky or even close to personal."

He looked so ticked off that Rachel knew she'd

taken a wrong turn. Her brain searched for answers and lit on one that seemed remotely plausible. If she was right, maybe there was a chance she *could* earn enough money to get her across the country. "I know. You have a wife. Maybe children. You need a housekeeper and maybe…you want a family portrait? Because yes, I can absolutely do that for you. I can take photos of your family." And she would charge extra this time, enough to earn her way to Maine. Where she would figure out the next logical step. Hopefully.

Unfortunately, Shane was looking at her as if she'd just said something obscene. "No family of any kind. No people. Things. I'm selling a ranch and all its furnishings and machinery. Everything has to go, down to the nails in the floor. There'll be an auction, maybe some bits and pieces offered on the internet. I just need someone to help get the house in saleable condition. And someone to take a few photos to help market the place. If you can do both, that's a bonus, because I have an extremely short time to hire people, pull this all together and get this deal done."

"I see."

"You don't, but it doesn't matter. Do you have time? Would you consider taking on a job? I can make it worth your while. Unless…"

She waited.

"Maybe you have to get back home?"

Well, she had to get away from here, and now that she'd set her sights on Maine she needed to look for work there, but it didn't have to be this minute. In fact, a little advance planning and money wouldn't be a bad idea, and this job Shane Merritt was offering looked to be her best bet to gain some breathing room and perspective and get her where she wanted to go. Still, Rachel knew better than to simply accept a man's word.

She dialed Ruby's number, completing it this time. Carefully, she explained that she had gotten a recommendation for Ruby from Angie at the diner, but she had gotten lost. She had a chance for a ride with someone named Shane Merritt.

"Shane Merritt?" The woman yelled Shane's name so loud that Rachel's eardrums cried out in pain. She held the phone away from her ear and punched on the speakerphone. "Shane Merritt is back in town? That wicked, heartless devil."

Rachel blinked. Shane, amazingly enough, didn't look even remotely surprised or upset. "You think I'd be crazy to get a ride from him, then?"

"He's trouble, all right."

That didn't sound promising. "So I should say no?"

There was a pause. "Tell me, does he still look as sinfully gorgeous as ever? Like you'd just like to lick him from top to bottom?"

Rachel's eyes locked with Shane's. She felt her face turning warm as blood rushed in. She punched off the speakerphone.

"He looks…he looks pretty good. Healthy, I'd say." She knew she was blushing even more as she struggled to get out of this mess.

"Hmm," Ruby said. "I guess that's one way of putting it."

"I—do you even have a room you can rent me?" Rachel asked, stumbling on.

"I do. I surely do. So, Shane's going to drive you here. Man, I haven't seen him in years. That jerk." Ruby's voice seemed to vacillate between excitement and anger. "He was always trouble and always *in* trouble, too. Plus, he was hardheaded, obstinate, slippery. Bad, unreliable, especially where women were concerned. Heartless. With you and making you feel loved one day and gone the next. Bad."

"I see," Rachel said quietly. "So I shouldn't ride with him?"

"What? Oh. No, hon, go ahead and ride with him. I've got no way to get you here. Just don't trust him to stick. He'll hurt you bad."

Rachel nodded, then remembered that Ruby couldn't see her. "All right. Thank you." She hung up the phone and looked at Shane.

"She says you're bad."

He shrugged.

"She says you're slippery and obstinate."

"Is that a problem? This is a short-term job. I'll be your boss. Obstinate comes with the territory." He stared at Rachel unflinchingly, and that direct gaze of his made her feel too exposed. As if he knew her thoughts and that much of her bravado was a bluff. Still, he had a point. They were talking about working together, not dating.

"Not a problem," she agreed.

"Good." The word was clipped. He looked impatient. For some reason impatient looked very sexy on him. Rachel reminded herself that Ruby had told her not to trust him.

Good advice. Especially because this man, this Shane person, looked…kind of angry. She could tell that he wasn't totally enthused about hiring her. Maybe he'd had no choice. Finding temporary employees in a town this small might be a challenge. Strangely, his lack of enthusiasm made her feel slightly safer. At least she would have no false expectations, unlike her experience with Dennis.

"So…you're going to give me a ride to Ruby's?"

"Yes." Obviously, he was a man of few words. That might be a good thing. Less interaction. If only he didn't look so…so…*virile.* Rachel frowned at the word, her tension and discomfort rising again.

"What if I decide not to work for you?" she asked suddenly, and immediately wanted to smack herself. After all, had any other jobs dropped out of the sky? No, but this man…this overwhelming man who stared at her as if could read the secrets and fears she kept locked away inside her…

Rachel swallowed hard. *Try to look nonchalant,* she ordered herself. *Try to look as if you don't even see him as a man.*

"You'll get a ride no matter what," he said.

"Because you don't want me on your conscience." Why was she pushing this, trying to peg the man's motives? No doubt because she was tired and frustrated and just plain mad as heck. Mostly at herself for being naive and impulsive and ending up stranded and broke. She hated feeling that all of her choices and power had been taken from her. And she needed to see things clearly and not miss things this time.

"I don't." And there was something in his eyes, some pained look, that told her that those words had meaning, too. He frowned. "So, does that mean that you're not taking the job? You didn't exactly say no, but you also haven't said yes."

She looked him directly in the eye. "Yes." A frisson of awareness slid through her. Saying yes to this man— this bad man, she corrected, remembering Ruby's warnings—might not be the smartest thing she'd ever done, and she needed to be smart.

"Despite Ruby's warnings?"

She lifted her chin defiantly. "I don't care how bad you are, because this is just going to be about work."

"Not a chance of anything more," he agreed.

Another woman might have been offended, but not Rachel. When a man said no, he was most likely being honest.

"And just so we're clear," he said, "I mentioned that I had a limited time frame. The truth is that this job won't last more than three weeks. I can't stay longer than that."

"I don't need more time than that. I just need enough money to get me out of here."

"All right." He held out his hand. "We have a deal then?"

Rachel stared for just a second. His hand was large, very male, with long, strong fingers. She slipped her palm against his and he—very briefly—closed his hand over hers. Warmth moved from his skin to hers in a most disturbing way that made her too aware that she was a woman and this was an overwhelming male she had just committed her time to. "A deal."

And then he released her just as quickly as he'd touched her.

Don't trust ricocheted through her mind, but she didn't have to be reminded. Not after today.

Hours later, on a narrow bed, staring at the moon, Rachel shivered, remembering all that had happened today. Her relationship with Dennis had been a horrible mistake, and she hadn't seen it coming. She knew it was because he'd made her feel that her skill with a camera made her stand out from the crowd in a good way, something she wasn't used to. She'd been naive. Now her eyes were clearer. She duly noted that there was a good chance that agreeing to work for someone like Shane would prove to be a mistake.

If she let it. "But I won't. I'll be on my guard," Rachel promised herself. Besides, it wasn't as if doing a little cleaning and taking a few pictures for some rancher was going to change her life.

CHAPTER TWO

"I PROMISE that I'll pay you for letting me stay here as soon as I can," Rachel said, drying a cup and putting it in the cabinet Ruby directed her to. She tried not to listen for the sound of Shane's car coming down the road. For some reason the prospect of riding in a car again with a man that potent had her spooked. Still, it was probably just a delayed reaction to her situation and the stress of yesterday. Nothing at all to do with the man.

Unfortunately, Ruby had noticed her nervousness. And misinterpreted it.

"Don't worry," she told Rachel. "He'll probably be here on time. When he was young, he was bull-headed and full of 'I dare you to make me try to do that.' If you put your foot down and demanded that he do something, he was almost sure to do the exact opposite. And he was a fighter. That landed him in jail a time or two. But I'm sure he's different now. He's a successful businessman, and since he was always a mathematical genius I'm sure he must spend some time on work and not so much on raising hell or loving up women."

The image of a half-naked Shane on a bed immediately sprang into Rachel's mind. She frowned. What was wrong with her?

Stop that right now, she ordered herself. She didn't even like the man. She didn't *want* to like the man. Hadn't she just yesterday shed one bad example of the male species?

Rachel shuddered. For two years, ever since Jason had broken her heart by leaving her for "a womanly woman," the woman he'd been waiting for all his life, as he put it, she'd sworn off associations with men entirely. Now she seemed to be making up for lost time, hooking up with one untrustworthy male after another. The thought that she might be turning into her mother, going gooey and giddy over any man who wandered near her, made Rachel feel suddenly sick.

She grabbed another cup and forced herself not to attack it. She needed to keep her mind on the work she'd been lucky enough to find, even if it was work she wasn't really qualified to do. She'd already nearly burned Ruby's boarding house down by trying to help her cook. That couldn't happen with Shane. Nothing bad could happen with Shane or he would fire her rear end.

Don't let that happen, she ordered herself. *Be professional. Just professional.*

"So, he's good with numbers?" Rachel said. "Kind of an accountant type?" That sounded safe. Good.

Ruby laughed. "If you're thinking you can take the edge off of a man like Shane by slapping a label on him, good luck with that. He'll still be just as much of a heartbreaker. Besides, he's got those smoldering eyes."

He did. "I hadn't noticed."

Her comment was followed immediately by the sound of a car door slamming, and Rachel nearly dropped a cup. In less than a minute those smoldering eyes were staring at her and Ruby. He hadn't knocked, but then, this *was* an inn.

"Ready?" Shane asked in that deep voice of his.

No. But that was the wrong answer. "Yes, just as soon as I finish up here. I owe Ruby big-time."

"That's okay. You run along," Ruby said.

At the same time Shane said, "All right. I'll wait."

"Thank you," Rachel said in her best prim employee voice.

"Well, then, did you eat already, Shane?" Ruby asked.

"I did."

"Could you eat again? If you had to make your own breakfast, you probably ate something disgusting."

A brief but wide smile flitted across Shane's face, revealing those devastating dimples before it disappeared. Rachel tried not to stare, sure that Ruby was watching her to see her reaction. No man should be allowed to look that good.

"I wouldn't want to trouble you."

"If your memory hasn't failed you, you'll know that there's always something on the stove here. Sit down and eat."

Shane moved toward the table. "Thank you."

Uh-oh, Rachel thought. Shane was a big eater and Ruby was a really good cook. What would he think when he had to eat Rachel's cooking? How soon would he fire her? She hoped she could at least make a few dollars before that happened. Maybe enough to get her a few miles closer to her destination.

Behind her, she could hear the clatter of dishes and the sound of a chair scraping against the floor as Shane sat down behind her. Rachel rubbed the dishes dry. When she was finished, she turned around to find

Shane already waiting for her. This time when he asked if she was ready she couldn't put off the inevitable.

Rachel Everly wasn't thrilled about this job. That much was clear to Shane as they got in his truck and drove toward the ranch. He'd never seen anyone take so much time drying a dish.

Not that he blamed her. If he'd been caught flat broke and forced to earn his way home he wouldn't be thrilled, either. Plus, Ruby was a colorful storyteller. There was no telling what she had told Rachel. There were plenty of stories circulating about him, and he didn't exactly shine in any of them. Some of them dealt with things he didn't want to think about. Most, if not all of them, were true.

Not that Rachel's enthusiasm for the task mattered. It was just a job that needed to be done, and the sooner they waded in, the sooner both of them could be free of the ranch, Moraine and each other. They might as well hit the ground running.

"You might want to pay attention to which direction we're headed," he said after a few minutes. "Some of these country roads aren't marked all that well, and it's easy to get turned around. You'll need to know how to get back to Ruby's."

He felt rather than saw her turn to him. "Is it close enough to get there on foot?"

"Only if you're a horse and you have a lot of time." Shane might not want to get to know this woman, but the fact that she had a habit of saying things that forced him to hold back his smile wasn't a good thing. He'd meant it when he'd said he didn't want there to be anything personal about this situation. He was here to cut the final cords that bound him to this place, and when he left he never wanted to look back again. So, there was no way he'd allow himself to do anything he might regret. Not this time.

"I don't understand," she said.

"You need to know the area, because there may be times when I'll be out on the far reaches of the ranch and won't be able to drive you back to Ruby's when it's time for you to go home. Or you might need to pick up supplies. At any rate, there are a lot of vehicles at the ranch. Hopefully, we'll find one that'll run and you can borrow it. Do you drive stick?"

There was a slight hesitation. "I do now."

"That'll do. I'll show you the basics."

He felt rather than saw her nod. "And you'll be very specific about what my job entails, won't you?"

"It pretty much just entails basic cleanup work and a few photos."

"And cooking, Mr. Merritt." She was clutching the handle of the door.

He frowned. "Shane. Just Shane. I'm not sure what Ruby told you, but I know she's a good storyteller and a romantic. Just so you know, you've got nothing to fear from me. I really meant it when I said that there would be nothing personal involved in this job."

Now he had her attention. She sat up straighter. "I never thought otherwise."

"You're practically ripping the handle off the door."

Immediately she released it as if it were on fire. "Sorry. I guess it's just being in unfamiliar territory. I'm a city girl and I've never been on a ranch."

"I see." But, remembering her rather magnificent tirade in the street yesterday and her long walk down the empty road, she didn't strike him as the type who was afraid of grass, fences and trees. Still, given the fact that she was stuck in Moraine and broke, she had other reasons to want to hold on tight to something, he supposed. Not that it was any of his concern.

"And in case it wasn't clear yesterday," she said, interrupting his thoughts, "you don't have to worry about me, either. I'll be totally professional. I'm not the type who has romantic notions. I'm not pining for a cowboy. I don't date people I work with. For the foreseeable future, I'm not dating anyone. If I'm slightly tense, it has nothing to do with anything Ruby may have said. I'm just getting my bearings."

"Point taken. I apologize for thinking that Ruby might have told you something that made you apprehensive."

She turned toward him then, her dark hair brushing across her cheek. He had a feeling she wanted to tell him that she wasn't afraid of anything.

"Excuse me, but Ruby said… Have you really been in jail?" she asked, surprising him.

As if a door had been opened, old bad memories rushed in. "Yes." No point in denying it, but he knew his tone said *back off.*

"Sorry. That was pretty rude of me, but I needed to know," she said. "I have a bad habit of being slightly impulsive and too direct. *Probing* is the way one person put it."

Great. He'd wanted an uncomplicated quick fix and he'd ended up with a woman who was going to pry into parts of his life that were open to no one, including himself.

"I'll work on curbing that. Just tell me if I get out of line," she said.

"Don't worry. I will." That was a promise.

For some reason, despite his grating tone, she seemed

to relax a bit, studying the landscape. They passed the timbered entrance gates to the Bella Bryce Ranch. A few miles down the road were the modest iron gates of the Regal R. Shane could sense Rachel's curiosity, though she kept silent. But when he turned in at Oak Valley, with its huge timbers with carved oak leaves climbing up and curling around the letters, she turned to him. "This looks big. It's all yours?"

Somehow that made it sound too personal. "Yes, I'm the sole owner of Oak Valley Ranch." Which was all wrong. He'd never wanted it, it should never have been his, and there were plenty of people who would agree with him on that.

"And yet you're selling it?"

Her voice was incredulous. He tried not to frown, but it was difficult. He didn't want to have to explain the whys and wherefores, what his life had been like growing up here, what had happened later and why he could never stay.

"I guess," she said, "if you lived in a place all your life, this would seem like no big deal?" Clearly she was trying to deal with his frown. "And even though this is your home—"

"It's not my home." His voice came out a bit too harsh.

His comment was met by silence. *Idiot.* Why had he cut her off and said something that made this seem even more personal? She was just here to do a job. He wasn't going to expose her to his history.

"I lived here most of my life, ever since I was three, but I've been gone for ten years and these days I run a business that keeps me on the move. I live in a lot of different places." He hoped that explanation was enough to satisfy her.

"That works for you? Living in so many different places?"

Yes. Hell, yes. "It suits me perfectly. I was made to be on the move."

"Not me," she said, shaking her head, her long dark curls sliding against her shoulders. "Not at all. The one thing I want is my very own home in my favorite place. Maine. Same place all the time."

He chanced a closer look at her and found that she had turned toward him. Those pretty brown eyes were intense, more than he would have expected given her casual lead-in questions. What must have happened to her to cause that kind of raw longing for a roots-buried-deep home of her own?

His curiosity must have been written on his face, because an enticing trace of pink painted her cheeks and dipped deep into the collar of her white shirt. Immediately a smoky trail of heat slipped through his body.

That wasn't good. He was her boss. She was his employee. He needed to start acting more like an employer and help her get her bearings.

"You said you were a city girl. So, if you have any questions, feel free to ask."

"About ranching?"

"About whatever you need to know."

"You might be sorry you said that."

He had no doubt she was right. He'd seen Rachel in action, stranding herself in Moraine when a man had wronged her. She'd been magnificent, but perhaps a bit impulsive. He'd already been treated to one or two of her more impulsive questions. And he had fences. High fences with padlocks.

"There's a good chance I might not answer every question in the way you'd like," he warned.

She nodded. "That's okay. You're my boss. You're allowed to tell me to slow down, to stop. You can tell me no."

There was that dreaded heat again. Shane wanted to groan. *No* wasn't the word he thought of when he looked at her. Certainly not *slow down.*

It occurred to him that he probably hadn't been dating enough of late if he was having these kinds of erotic thoughts about a woman who made him cringe with half of what came out of her mouth. It also occurred to him that he was going to have to watch himself. She was in his care now. That made him responsible for her well-being, and having the wrong kinds of thoughts about her wasn't allowed. The good thing was that their relationship wouldn't last long.

He only hoped she was going to get the house in order quickly, had some skills with that camera, and knew her way around a stove.

Rachel wished she could relax a bit. Discovering that she and her boss had different goals had been freeing, but she was still far too aware of him. Maybe it had something to do with the emptiness of the land they were traversing. She and Shane appeared to be the only two people within miles.

The thing was, she'd meant it when she'd told him that she wasn't a romantic. She'd been very young when she'd first learned that relationships weren't made to last forever and that a promise given wasn't necessarily a promise kept. Her grown up relationships had only served as more proof.

But, darn it, there was just something about Shane

that made a woman want to…to look at him. Closely. It was disconcerting. She had never been a very physical kind of woman. Lust had not been a part of her life. The fact that she was even having these kinds of thoughts was totally alarming.

So don't look. Get to work, she ordered herself. *Do something to create some distance.*

"So, Mr. Merritt, you have three weeks. What needs to be done during that time?" she asked casually, just as if she hadn't been thinking about what Shane looked like underneath his shirt.

He raised a brow. "Shane," he said, correcting her once again."

She nodded. "Got it. Shane." So much for distance.

"The ranch has been vacant for a while," he said. "Things have deteriorated. The hay didn't get cut, so that has to be done and then reseeded. At a minimum, fences have to be mended, buildings have to be repaired, irrigation systems checked out, weeds controlled. As I mentioned earlier, the house needs cleaning. The place has to look inviting if I'm going to be able to sell it quickly, and it has to be sold. Once it's in marketable condition, I'll ask you to take a few photos. We'll list it anywhere we can and end with an open house, followed by an auction if we haven't had any offers before then. Basically, we're getting the ranch show ready, not necessarily ranch-ready."

"The hay is for show?"

"Hay in the field will be more attractive. It's one less thing the new owners will have to worry about when winter comes and they need to feed their animals."

Rachel nodded. Once the two of them stopped talking, that sense of being alone with Shane in a world

separated from everything else hit her again. "It's so
quiet here other than the birds," she said. "You don't
seem to have any animals. No cows or sheep or…what-
ever else a ranch has. I don't know. Llamas? Bison?
Doesn't a ranch have to have animals? Aren't they
what make a ranch…a ranch?"

He almost smiled that devastating smile, but—thank
goodness—he put it away before she'd even gotten a
good look. "Yes, most ranches have animals, but this
one is for sale, and no one's been here since…it's been
a while." She didn't miss that slight stumble, or the
momentary pain that had flared in his eyes.

"When I inherited the ranch, I wasn't prepared to
deal with the situation, so I just let things sit for the
most part. Except you can't just let cattle sit unat-
tended. I hired someone to sell them off."

"All of them?"

"All the cattle, yes. As for the horses…"

"Of course. You had horses, too."

"I still have them." He looked a bit sheepish at that.
"I wanted to personally handle that bit, so I had them
stabled in the next county."

"Is it nicer in the next county? Better grass or something? I mean…I know I don't know anything about
ranching, but…why there when there were all those
ranches we passed?"

He shrugged. "You were right. Better grass."

She could tell he was lying and that he didn't care
if she knew it. He obviously had a reason and she, as
his employee, wasn't entitled to it. Rachel zipped her
lips. She had probably been talking too much, asking
too many questions. It was a bad habit she'd developed
early in life, the result of having to get to know large
groups of people quickly.

Still, as they came over a rise and she saw a building in the distance, she couldn't help asking, "Is that it? The house…or…? I don't know much about ranches. Aren't there sometimes multiple buildings?"

"There are other buildings, but none of this size. Yes, that's the house." There didn't seem to be an ounce of pride in his voice.

Rachel understood why as they drew closer. She felt she should say something, but she wasn't quite sure what to say without sounding critical. "It's…it's an impressive building," she tried, which was no lie. In fact, it must have been very impressive at one time. A long, sprawling white building that looked as if it had been added onto multiple times, it dominated the land and looked out onto the mountains. But the paint was barely there, the chimneys were crumbling and there were porch boards that had worn through. A lone shutter clung to the side of one window, dangling at a crooked angle.

Shane stopped the truck, and he and Rachel got out. They walked up to the house and he opened the door, reaching around her. His arm brushed her sleeve, ever so slightly, and it was all she could do not to suck in a deep breath. Just that one little touch had called up such a giant reaction in her. How ridiculous. How unlike her. How unnerving.

Get your act together, Rachel, she ordered.

"My apologies." Had the darn man read her thoughts?

"No big deal," she said, as if his nearness didn't even affect her. "Could you…? If this is going to be my workspace, I'd like to see the rest of the house, please."

"Prepare yourself," was his response. And when she stepped over the threshold, Rachel understood why.

They took a quick tour, their steps ringing off the wood in the cavernous emptiness of most of the house. Dust and cobwebs lay over everything Shane hadn't already touched. There were no curtains at the windows, and one of the panes was broken. In the rooms that were furnished, Rachel noted that the furniture had probably been old when Shane was a boy. The kitchen appliances might have appeared in old horror movies, and all of the light fixtures looked questionable. Despite the condition of the house, or maybe because of it, Shane was moving quickly and they had soon covered all but one of the rooms. "I just want to fix it enough to sell it," he said.

"How about this room?" she asked, nodding toward the one room they hadn't gone in.

"Don't worry about that one," he said. "It was my younger brother Eric's."

Rachel smiled. "You think he's going to mind if I take a peek?"

Shane trapped her gaze with his own. "No. The ranch belonged to him. Now it's mine."

And he had apparently inherited it, which meant that his brother was dead.

Rachel wanted to drop her gaze. She didn't. "I'm sorry for your loss." She didn't say that she was sorry for her light comment. She hadn't known. He hadn't told her.

"I'm sorry, too," was all he said. "We'll leave that room alone for now."

But eventually, if he was going to sell the house—and he'd made it clear that he was—even that room would have to be fixed.

"Your call," she said. "You're the boss."

"Where that room is concerned...yes." And she was

only the employee. It would be good to remember that and not ask too many questions or get carried away. In any way. For once in her life she should learn to keep her mouth shut and not go poking at things with sticks. Because it was a good bet that if she poked Shane she might get a reaction she couldn't handle.

"Not going to happen," she muttered beneath her breath.

"Excuse me?" She looked up to find herself pinned by those awesome, fierce eyes.

"It looks as if there's a lot that needs to be done before you'll want to have an open house, even if you're only going for show ready," she said. And there was no hiding from the fact that she had zero experience of the types of things he needed doing. Her life had been a lot of moving. There'd never been a home she could call her own, let alone take care of. Her food had mostly been institutional, and when it hadn't been it had still been prepared by someone else.

"Rachel?"

She looked up into Shane's silver-blue eyes and saw…concern. Uh-oh. She'd shown her hand, hadn't she?

"Yes?" The word came out a bit too soft.

She almost thought he swore beneath his breath. He was standing so close she had to look up. She could feel his warmth. His gaze passed over her, and she could barely breathe.

"If you've decided you don't want the job, tell me now."

Oh, no. Here she'd trusted him and already he was firing her. "I need the job," she said, hoping she didn't sound too pathetic.

"Fair enough. I'll help with the heavy lifting."

The thought of having him in close proximity lifting things for her made her palms feel clammy. She felt awkward and fidgety. "I know I'm short, but I'm capable of doing this myself," she said, but she didn't know who she was trying to convince. Him or herself.

And, since she had punctuated her sentence by swiping a finger across a bit of woodwork in a dramatic swoop, she now had dust all over her fingers. She started to close her hand into a fist so that he wouldn't see what an idiot she'd been, but it was too late. Shane pulled a navy bandana from his pocket, cupped her hand in his own much larger one and gently wiped the dust away.

When he released her, her hand tingled, even though he had barely touched her.

It occurred to her that working with Shane would be a much bigger challenge than how to approach these chores she was so ill prepared for. Still, if she could bulldoze her way through and do the job quickly, if he could sell this place fast, she could get back to civilization and Maine, where there were no dangerous cowboy bosses. She hoped.

"Ever been to Maine?" she asked.

"Your favorite place," he remarked.

"Yes. And it's also my future, the place I intend to build my dreams."

He nodded at that. "I wish you luck. I really do, even though I'm not a big believer in dream-building. I'm strictly practical. As for Maine, I've been there, but not in years. No reason to show up there anymore."

Rachel felt a little pool of relief slip right through her. She would never cross paths with Shane once she left here. Oh, yes. Maine was looking better every minute.

CHAPTER THREE

"I'LL move everything out of the dining room so you can get started in there in a little bit, but for now let's take care of transportation for you," Shane said. It was time to move things along. Just dive in and get the preliminaries over so that he and Rachel could start the job in earnest. The sooner they started, the sooner they ended.

"That works for me," she said.

That seemed like a pretty enthusiastic response, considering how much had happened to her during the last day and given the terrible condition of the house. It had been going downhill ever since his mother had died many years ago, but he just hadn't cared. Now he had to, for several reasons. One of them was standing beside him, looking pale and scared but determined. He was lucky Rachel hadn't run out the door screaming. Many women—or men—would have walked rather than face this disaster.

He was grateful that she hadn't asked him more about Eric's room. He had taken everything that had belonged to his mother and Eric and locked the past away in that room. Sooner or later he'd have to face those memories, but not today. Or tomorrow. Or any day real soon.

"This way to the garage," he said as she followed him. "So driving stick will be a new experience for you? All right, let's see what we can find that you'll like."

"I'm not fussy. Dependable is more important than anything, I'd guess. You have some long, lonely stretches of road."

"Good point. Dependable it is." He led her out to a big gray building and pulled open the wide double doors.

For a second there was silence, just the birds and the insects chirping away. "Um…there are ten cars here," Rachel said.

"I know."

"That one in the back looks as if it's from another era."

"It is. It's a Duesenberg. Probably doesn't run very well."

She gave him a look. "Isn't that some sort of collector's item?"

"For those who collect, yes."

"And it's sitting there covered in cobwebs?"

"That's about the shape of it."

Rachel tilted her head, looking at him quizzically. "What?" he asked.

"Nothing. Just…I've known some people with money in my lifetime. Most of them like to flaunt it. If one of them had a Duesenberg they would be bringing it up in conversations, maybe have a print of it hanging somewhere in the house."

Shane shrugged. The Duesenberg had been his stepfather's pride and joy. Next to the ranch, of course. "I'm not much into collecting cars." Or ranches.

"Fair enough. What are you into?"

Kissing women with pretty brown eyes that snap when the woman is angry or nervous or that sparkle when the woman is amused. Stupid thought.

Keep it simple, Merritt, he reminded himself. *No complications. This woman is the serious type. That makes her off-limits.*

"Not a collector at all. I'm more into the working parts."

She looked suddenly self-conscious. Had he said something suggestive? Maybe he had, given how low his voice had dropped. "Of a car, that is. Engines. Systems. How things are engineered. The technical stuff." He flipped open the hood on the nearest car. "Not exactly looking good here." And neither were any of the others. "But I think I can get one of these two to run." He gestured toward the black sedan and the red sports car.

"Black is very practical and so is a sedan," she said. But somehow he could practically see her dancing on her toes when she looked at the sports car.

"I've always been partial to red myself," he found himself saying. *Why had he said that? What was that about? He was not a guy who gave a lot of weight to the color of his car, and given the choice of black or red he probably would have chosen black every time.*

"I don't know. Red seems flashy. I'm just the house-keeper. I should be practical."

"Are you always practical?"

As if he'd turned on a switch, she flushed straight down to the roots of those pretty brown tresses. "Not especially. Hardly ever."

Ah, now he saw. She'd been lectured about it, too, he was pretty sure. He wondered if that guy she'd been with had been the one who'd chided her about her impractical tendencies. "I'm fairly confident that the red one is in better shape." He wasn't. Not at all. And why was he doing this?

No clue. Certainly not because he was interested in the woman. That wasn't true. At all. Was it? Maybe it was just because if he thought about Rachel's situation he wouldn't have to think about his own and how being back here was like walking over eggshells filled with bad memories. If he didn't tread lightly, the shells would break and the memories would spill out. Concentrating on Rachel was easier, especially since there was no chance he'd ever get close enough to her to turn her into another bad memory. Yeah, that was probably it.

"Let's get the car running," he suggested.

In the end he had to make a phone call to Somesville in the next county for a rush delivery of a new battery, some spark plugs and fluids. In spite of the fact that he hadn't looked under the hood of a car since he'd left Moraine, all those years of keeping the engines here running had done the trick and he was sure that there was nothing major wrong with the cars. The biggest problem once he'd started appeared to be Rachel herself.

"Let me help, Shane. This is ridiculous. You're lending me a car, and here I am just standing around being useless. What can I do to help? Show me."

He looked at her pale blue slacks and white blouse and then at the greasy rag he was holding. "You'll get dirty."

She got a grim look on her face. "I'm not just some helpless female who fears dirt and spends all her time primping to make people think I look good." Then she put her hands on her hips and all he could think about for several seconds was how curvy her hips were and how good she really did look.

"I never said you were like that," he said, frowning at his own too-male reaction.

For one brief second she looked chagrined. "Sorry. You didn't. It's just that…I've known a few of those women. I…let's just say that it's a pet peeve of mine. And, really, I want to lend a hand. You're my boss. I should help."

"All right. Let's see what we can find to keep the grease off you." He began to open the drawers to the storage cabinets looking for some old shop aprons that might still be lying around. The cabinets were disorganized, not quite as bad as the house, but close.

"How about this?" Rachel asked, and he looked up to see that she was holding a pair of coveralls. Eric's old coveralls.

His heart felt as if someone had just punched him straight in the chest. He opened his mouth to tell her no, but Rachel was already shimmying into the royal blue coveralls, sliding them up over the curve of her hips.

All his objections died in his throat. Every cell in his body went on alert. Everything that was male in him stopped and paid attention as the coveralls that were meant for a stick-straight small male conformed to the perfect roundness of Rachel's rear end, the aged and worn soft material causing it to cling to her in places. The right places—no, the wrong places for a man trying to stay aloof…and sane. For several seconds Shane thought he might have stopped breathing.

And then it got worse. She reached back to find the sleeves, and there was no way he couldn't notice the soft curve of her breasts. It didn't matter that the legs of the coveralls were too long, that she had to roll up the sleeves or that the things barely touched her in places once she was inside them. As she raised the zipper, covering herself, he realized that he hadn't spoken through the whole ordeal…and that he was acting like a man who'd never seen a woman's body before.

Quickly, he ducked under the hood of the car, just barely missing banging his head. "Here," he said, holding out an oil wrench.

To his surprise, city girl Rachel jumped in with both feet. She slid under the dirty car and asked him to explain the basics of emptying the oil pan and removing the filter. She insisted on helping with the spark plugs and the new battery.

When they were done, he looked down to find her smiling. "You'd think we were doing something exciting," he mused.

"It was new for me, and I got one-on-one training. People pay big bucks to take classes in this very thing in my world."

It was the perfect opening to ask a question, find out more about her, discover what her world was like. But he wasn't going there. It was better that he not know too much about her. He needed to keep things impersonal.

"Besides, when I finally make it back to Maine and save enough money to get my own little dream house, maybe with a little clunker car of my own, I might need to know this stuff."

Another perfect opening. He firmed his mouth into a straight line and refused to ask about her dreams. Instead, he simply nodded.

She didn't seem to notice his silence. "But you," she said. "I'm amazed at people who can do what you've just done. You seem to be very good at this," she said, stepping over that line he had laid down and aiming straight for the personal information.

He frowned. "I've done it a lot." But not since he'd left the ranch.

"Is this kind of thing part of your business?"

"Changing the oil in cars?"

Perhaps he'd sounded too incredulous, since the result was a pretty blush that crept up Rachel's neck. This time he refused to look at where the blush disappeared into her coveralls. Not that it mattered. His imagination kicked in as he wondered just how far that blush traveled down her body before he managed to order himself to stop.

"I guess the answer is no," she said. "Ruby said you were very successful. I just thought…you know…do what you love, do what you know…"

"Makes sense," he agreed. "But I run a consulting firm that teaches companies how to use technology more efficiently."

"Oh, yes, the mathematical genius thing Ruby talked about."

"That was always an exaggeration." And it had often been a criticism. Apparently Rachel agreed with the criticism part. Her brow was furrowed.

"Not into math?" he asked, breaking his own rule about personal questions less than a minute after he'd resolved to steer clear of anything that drew them closer to each other in any way. What was it about Rachel that led a man to forget his own rules?

"It's not my best skill," she agreed, "but I admire those who know how to tame numbers and make them do what they want them to. I was just…" Her blush grew. "It's nothing."

"Obviously it's something."

"Nothing important. I'm just divesting myself of another stereotype—the nerdy numbers guy who's not good with women. According to Ruby you've got a reputation with the women here and…"

He pinned her with his gaze, raised a brow.

"Right," she said. "Let's just leave it at that. Not the kind of thing most employees discuss with their bosses, anyway."

But it was becoming obvious to Shane that Rachel didn't have much in common with most employees. Given his inability to just ignore her, or compartmentalize his reaction to her, he probably shouldn't have hired her, but now that he had…

We move on, he thought. *Quickly. Very quickly.* Already he was beginning to associate her with the ranch and Moraine, two places he never intended to think of again once he was gone. Already he could see that she had the kind of dreams a man like him would never fit. The sooner they were through with each other the better.

Rachel had barely arrived back at Ruby's in her borrowed car when Angie from the diner showed up. "Word in town is that you're working for Shane. I just thought I'd better pop in and give you a warning. There will be questions."

Rachel blinked. "About what?"

Ruby and Angie exchanged a glance. "Well, some women will want to know whether he's as devastating as he used to be. Whether he makes you get that fluttery feeling inside when he turns those blue eyes on you and says your name in that deep voice."

"What? No!" Rachel said.

Another glance exchanged by the two women. Clearly they didn't believe her.

"All right, he's good-looking. I'll give you that," Rachel admitted. "And he's kind of...I don't know..."

"Sexy as hell?" Angie suggested. "Yes, I saw him in town. Time hasn't done him any harm. He's definitely swoon-worthy."

"He's attractive," Rachel said, a bit primly. "But I'm just his employee."

Ruby opened her mouth to speak.

"*Just* his employee," Rachel repeated. "I'm not looking for a man."

"Hmm," Angie said. "I heard you just got rid of a bad one yesterday, but Celia Truro said she got a look at that guy and he couldn't hold a candle to Shane in the looks department."

"I wasn't dating Dennis. I was working for him."

"I know, but still...he was the man you were with, and if he was a jerk, tearing him down just a little by comparing him to Shane wouldn't hurt you. Just sayin'."

Rachel tried to look offended, but she ended up smiling. "Okay, Dennis was a jerk, and he didn't have Prince Charming looks. In the end he didn't have Prince Charming anything."

"I know. I can't believe he dumped you right in the street," Ruby said.

"He didn't dump me. I dumped him."

"Good. You were smart to do it. I read a lot of romances. I meet a lot of men in my business," Angie said. "And a truly good man—no matter the relationship—would have at least insisted on giving you a ride to the nearest train, or made sure you had money, or at the very least called someone who could help you.

Heroes don't drive away and leave a woman stuck with no way to get home, no matter what the situation. You don't want to get mixed up with any bad men."

Exactly, Rachel thought, and both Shane and Ruby had already pegged Shane as a man who had done some bad things.

"Now for the even bigger question. Is it true Shane's selling Oak Valley?" Angie asked.

"That's what I'm here for. To help him get it ready to be sold."

Ruby shook her head. "That's a shame. That ranch was the best in the area in its day. He's selling the whole ranch?"

"Every cup and saucer, every blade of grass."

"Everything? I'd really love to see some of that stuff," Angie said. "I've met a few people who worked there for a short time. They said that Shane's mother had some fancy things."

"You've never been there?" Rachel asked.

Another look was exchanged by Ruby and Angie. "Shane's stepfather was a bit of a hermit. Not into having folks over."

"Well, Shane's having an open house when he puts the ranch on the market," Rachel offered.

The women's eyes lit up. "When?" they asked, almost in unison.

"Three weeks. Maybe a little less." After all, one day was already done, and she was pretty sure that if Shane managed to finish up all the work he wouldn't wait to put Oak Valley on the market.

"That's going straight on my calendar," Angie said.

"We'll be there," Ruby declared.

"Lots of people will be there," Angie said. "Oak Valley opening its doors? That will pull people in."

"Hopefully to buy the ranch," Rachel offered.

"Maybe." Ruby looked doubtful. "Not too many people around here who could afford a ranch that size. Most people will just want to see the place."

"And the women will want to drool over Shane," Angie added.

Uh-oh, Rachel thought. Maybe she should have asked Shane before she shared this information. Maybe he'd planned to keep his open house "by invitation only." She doubted he was going to be pleased to know that his new housekeeper had just invited the world to his doorstep to drool and paw.

She hadn't even done one ounce of work for him and already she had given the man a reason to fire her. Other than her utter lack of skills...which he would find out about tomorrow.

Focus, Rachel, focus, she ordered herself the next morning. *Keep your plan in mind. Shane Merritt has nothing to do with your plan, nothing to do with your future.* But she'd spent a good part of yesterday working beside him, and later sitting beside him as he'd coached her through the paces of learning to drive a stick shift.

"Like this?" she'd asked, wrestling with the shift.

"Like this," he'd said, covering her hand with his own as he'd moved the stick through the gears, showing her, guiding her.

Driving her crazy just because he was touching her, even though it was a completely impersonal touch.

"You are an idiot," she whispered between clenched teeth as she put Shane's lessons to use and drove all the way from Ruby's to the ranch, only lurching a little and only stalling the car twice. "Don't start getting any ideas about Shane. Don't you remember what Ruby told you? And don't you remember that you have golden plans for your future?"

Yes, she was finally going to be free to put down roots and have her own life exactly the way she had always wanted it. Where she wouldn't have to move all the time, where she might finally get the chance to settle down and have a real life on her own terms. Doing something as crazy as losing her mind over a man like Shane, who would mess with her dreams and who was so very wrong for a woman like her... Well, she knew better than most people what the consequences of that kind of idiocy would be.

Stop feeling things, she ordered herself.

Simple. Easy. Should be a breeze to pull off as long as she put her mind to it. But the minute she climbed out of the car and Shane walked toward her, all broad shoulders, long denim-clad muscular legs and smoldering eyes, easy flew right out the door.

"Something wrong?" she asked. "Did I...? I didn't get a scratch on your car or anything, did I? I was really careful to park it far away from all the others at the inn."

He shook his head. "The car's fine. You were driving real smooth, too."

An inordinate sense of pride welled up in Rachel and she started to smile. Until she remembered that those were the types of comments Dennis had made about her photos, and he had merely been trying to butter her up so he could use her. Not that there was any question about her being used this time. She was, after all, a hired employee, and as such, Shane was openly using her services...and paying her well for them. And then, too, a compliment was a compliment.

She'd been trained by the best in how to handle compliments.

"Thank you. I appreciate your role in my smooth driving," she said politely. And then, because she had sounded like some of the prim, prissy girls she had known in school, the ones she hadn't liked and who hadn't liked her, she rushed on, "So, there's no problem?"

"Just a holdup. One of the men I'd hired to help out broke his leg yesterday. For a while I thought I was going to have to ride out and look for someone new, but he managed to talk a friend into subbing for him. He'll be here later today. We're all set to get started. A full complement of ranch hands."

Rachel blinked. "Is that what I get to call myself? A ranch hand?" That was a title she'd never thought to own. A bit exotic, at least in the world she'd grown up in. She liked it. "Could be awesome."

He almost cracked a smile, almost showed her those amazing dimples, and he held out his hands in a submissive gesture. "Go for it. Knock yourself out."

"I intend to. Chance of a lifetime. So…I guess I should start tackling the ranch house?"

"I'll just be over at the barn repairing the roof. Shouting distance away and in plain sight if you need me. I'll see you at lunch." Then he was gone. And she was alone with the house.

"And I'm expected to make lunch," she reminded herself. Gulp. *Okay, okay, this is nothing.* Cleaning. Cooking. People did this all the time. Ordinary people did it, and she had always wanted to be just an ordinary person. The kind who lived in the same place all the time and took care of that place, because that was what ordinary people with homes of their own did. This was her chance to have that for a few weeks. She could do it. Shane was counting on her to do it.

So…first things first. Find a computer, look some stuff up. She had wanted to do that last night, but Ruby had been working on her books and Rachel owed her too much to ask her to stop her own work in order to let Rachel access the internet.

Now Rachel headed toward the office she remembered Shane showing her. On her way there she glanced out the window.

And saw Shane climbing off a ladder onto the roof of the barn. He stood there, all male, surveying his territory, a tool belt slung low on his hips. As she watched, he leaned into the tilt of the roof. Casually. Easily. As if he'd done this sort of thing before.

And then he took off his shirt and she saw bronzed muscles. She saw those broad shoulders. Naked.

Her mouth went dry.

At that moment Shane started to turn. In a second he would see her staring at him if he looked this way.

She let out a muffled squeak and jumped back away from the window. Without turning around again, she scurried toward the computer and plopped down in front of it. She stared at the screen.

And remembered what Shane had looked like standing there like the king of the ranch. All male all the time. Ranch guy. A man who could run a company, fix a car or mend a roof without even blinking. The kind of men women lusted over. The girls in the countless boarding schools she'd attended all her life would have gotten into shrieking, calculated battles over a man like that. Her mother would have set out to charm a man like that. And win him…until the newest husband material came along.

"And both of those are just two of the many reasons why you're not interested." She didn't ooze charm. She didn't want to. And anyway, Shane was clearly out of her league. He could have all those charming women, and apparently had already had many.

I'm the housekeeper, she reminded herself. *I'm on the road to my future, to my dream.* And she had better start giving some thought to that future real soon.

"Yeah, just as soon as I figure out the most efficient way to clean a house quickly and how to make something palatable for lunch." A man who had spent the morning pounding nails in a roof would probably have a big appetite when he came in all hot and sweaty.

Rachel tried not to imagine that moment. She hoped Shane had put his shirt back on by then. She hoped he'd be so tired he wouldn't notice any problems with the food.

But first she had to find some food to make and directions on how to make it. Her fingers flew over the keys, their clacking sounding a lot like...desperation.

When Shane walked back into the house, nothing looked that different from the way it had looked that morning...except there seemed to be a few computer printouts lying about. He looked at the one lying beneath the hallway mirror. The Best Way to Clean Mirrors and Windows it read. There was another one on the oak sideboard called How to Make Woodwork Glow along with One Hundred Uses for Vinegar and The Easiest Way to Get Grease Off a Stove. There were more, but just then he heard a loud clatter, followed by, "Juno and Jupiter and...and...oh, darn it!"

"Rachel?" He rushed into the kitchen.

She was standing at the stove, and she whirled

around when he appeared. Red sauce had splattered her white blouse, there were smudges of dust on her cheeks and the light that had been in her eyes this morning had dimmed. She looked...pained.

"Did you hurt yourself?" The words sounded like an accusation. He didn't mean them that way, but his mother's death had begun as an injury. And—no, he wasn't going there.

To stop his thoughts, he slid closer to her and took her hand. He looked her over, searching for burns from the sauce. He reached out and placed two fingers beneath her chin, turning her face from one side to the other. Searching since she still hadn't spoken.

"Rachel, could you please say something? I'm sorry I shouted."

"I can't even make spaghetti. Anyone can make spaghetti. Look, it says so right here," she said, holding up a sauce-splattered computer printout.

She gazed up at him with those big brown eyes that looked so sad and he wanted to waltz her back across the kitchen, lean her against the counter and kiss the sadness from her lips until they tilted up into her sunny smile again.

But that would be mad. It would be bad.

"Who says you can't make spaghetti?" he asked, sounding grumpier than he had intended.

She bit her lip. "I lied about knowing how to do this stuff," she said. "I hate people who lie. Dennis lied. And...lots of people have lied. But I don't. I hate that, but I did this time. I wanted the job."

"Well...wanting things makes everyone do things they regret later. I don't quite recall any lies from you, though." He had to say that, because even though he knew what she was talking about, he hated that forlorn look in her eyes, and he felt partially responsible. He'd suspected her secret and had hired her, anyway. He'd treated her to his frowns, he'd worried about his all-too-male reaction to her, and in an attempt to escape that reaction he'd left her to tackle something she had no experience with. Guilt assailed him, and he already knew way too much about guilt.

Plus, there was no excuse for him having left her feeling so stressed about her duties. As a man who'd trained many people, worked with many employees, he knew the drill. He understood how to make sure people were comfortable in their work before he left them alone to do their jobs.

But with Rachel…he'd walked away because she messed with his senses, wreaked havoc with his resolve. She distracted him, and he seriously couldn't afford to be distracted. Nonetheless—

"I implied that I could cook," she said, cutting into his thoughts. "And that I understood the secrets of housekeeping. I told you that I knew enough, and I tried to convince myself that it wasn't really a lie because *enough* is a relative word."

He couldn't help himself then. She sounded as if she'd just done something truly heinous. And, much as he wanted to build a rock-solid wall between them, to keep all smiles and interaction to a minimum, he couldn't stop himself from smiling. "It *is* a relative word."

"Don't you dare let me off the hook. I have standards, and if I expect others to adhere to them, I have to adhere to them, too."

"All right," he said quietly. "You're entitled to your standards. That's a nice motto to live by, I suppose."

"It's not my own. Ms. Drimmons, Sidson School,

Grade Five. I didn't even realize that I'd absorbed or... stolen her motto."

He smiled more. "Rachel, you don't have to confess *all* your supposed sins to me. Or any of them, for that matter. Plus, as far as sins go, using someone else's motto isn't a very big one. All right?"

"I know that, but put together with my lying—"

"Which I'm not concerned about and we're going to move past, providing you don't tell me any more lies. Anything else I should know?"

She shook her head.

"Okay, then, why don't we look at the spaghetti?"

"It's easy enough to see," she said, wearing that delicious blush he was beginning to look forward to. "There was something in the instructions about flinging a bit against the wall. I think I may have flung too much."

Shane looked to the wall opposite the stove. At least a dozen strands of spaghetti were either making their way down the wall or lying on the floor.

He couldn't keep the amused look off his face.

"It's not funny."

He raised an eyebrow.

"Okay," she conceded. "It is funny, but I'm not laughing."

And then she was chuckling. And so was he. Shane realized that this was the first time he'd laughed since his return to Oak Valley. It felt like a release valve, helping him breathe. And while he knew it was a temporary release, because nothing had changed, for the moment it was welcome.

"Come on, I'll bet the spaghetti is entirely edible." He started toward the stove and she followed him. "The sauce is a little burned on the bottom, because the heat was a little high, but what's on top will be fine."

"I could probably make a meal out of what's on my shirt."

Okay, he could not let that pass, even though everything that was smart and good told him not to look at her shirt.

He looked…and was rewarded with that glorious, enticing blush again. He also realized that she was right. A lot of the sauce had bubbled out of the pan and plopped onto her shirt.

"I'll lend you one of mine," he said. And this time he did the right thing. He locked his senses down and didn't try to imagine Rachel wearing the same shirt that lay against his skin every week.

Instead he handed her a colander to drain the pasta. "Let's eat."

She hesitated. "You're being very generous. I hardly made any headway on the house, and this isn't the meal you had every right to expect. Why aren't you firing me?"

He hesitated. He didn't want to examine his motives too closely. But an answer that was just as true as any other reason slipped out. "You're trying, you're working. That's the truth, and…there's one more truth."

She looked up at him, waiting.

"For reasons I don't want to discuss, I never wanted to come back to Oak Valley and Moraine. Being here is barely tolerable. But…you're an incredibly interesting person. You distract me from things I don't want to think about."

And now those brown eyes widened. "I…distract you?"

"Yes." He wasn't saying more. He'd said too much. He hoped he hadn't been wrong to tell her that.

"Shane?"

"Let's eat," he said, changing the subject. "And then let's get back to work. This afternoon I might need you to take some photos. I assume you do know how to use that Hasselblad?"

Good. She'd raised her chin. He preferred a defiant Rachel to a sad one. Sparring with her, he had to keep his wits about him. That kept him from thinking too much about touching her.

Rachel felt much calmer now that she was back on familiar territory. For half a second she wondered if Shane knew that and had thrown out the topic of photography to help her get her bearings. But, no, she had never shared just how passionate she was about photography with anyone, not even Dennis, who had been a photographer himself. She'd learned as a child that being overly passionate about something sometimes invited criticism, even laughter or derision. Still, she was grateful for the chance to do something she understood even if she still had a lot to learn before she would feel that she had even come close to mastering her craft.

"You're safe," she said. "I know how to take photos. I'm not a pro by a long shot, but you won't have to go looking for someone else as long as you don't need anything too involved."

"Just basic shots," he agreed.

"And these basic shots…they're of the barn you're working on? Of the house?"

"A few of those, and some of the other landmarks on the ranch. Also I'd like some of the horses." Had his voice warmed just a little? Maybe. Maybe not. His expression gave nothing away.

Rachel wasn't nearly as successful at concealing her feelings. "You're bringing the horses back?" She couldn't help smiling.

"You like horses?"

"I—I don't know. That is, of course I've seen them, and they're beautiful, but I've never actually spent time with any. Still, they'll add some life to the ranch, won't they? I mean…it's beautiful, but so quiet. Lonely."

"You don't like solitude?"

"I do. Sometimes." But not too much. She'd spent too much of her life alone, or essentially alone. When she finally settled in Maine she wanted neighbors and friends she could keep for the long haul. But she hadn't started this topic to discuss her own past or preferences. She'd been trying to be practical, for once.

"It just seems that a ranch would sell better and faster if it had horses," she said. She remembered what Ruby and Angie had said about there not being many potential buyers around here.

"You're probably right. And horses are more than just beautiful creatures who'll help sell the ranch. They're useful, loyal and more. I'll teach you to ride," he said with a sudden devastating smile.

Oh, boy, there it was, that guy Ruby had referred to, the one who could talk a girl out of her clothes and her common sense, even though she knew he didn't have a thing to offer her.

"For practical purposes," he clarified. "Eventually I'll want you to take a few photos of some of the more remote areas of the ranch where there are no roads."

A vision of herself and Shane riding side by side through a meadow, stopping to water their animals while he reached up and helped her from her horse, sliding her down the length of his body, came to her. Darn it, why did she suddenly feel so hot? Was she blushing? And why did she always have to have such a vivid imagination? It made her feel things she shouldn't feel and long for things that just weren't smart. Sometimes she craved impossible things. Like now.

Trying to shut down her imagination, she fell back on her years of boarding school training. She knew how to make polite responses in her sleep. "I'll look forward to it."

The part of her that had conjured up that ridiculously foolish vision agreed completely with her statement. But the part of her that insisted on reality and truth knew that, as enchanted as she was with the idea of horses and riding horses, Shane was never in this lifetime going to get her up on one of those mammoth creatures.

She sure hoped he had an ATV stashed in the back of the garage somewhere. If she had to get somewhere remote she could probably manage one of those.

But horses were definitely out. In a minute, or maybe in a day, she'd have to tell him that. That and the fact that all of Moraine was probably going to show up on his doorstep for the open house...if they didn't storm the ranch and arrive sooner. A sudden vision of scantily clad women trying to look inside Shane's house or get a glimpse of his muscles and blue eyes slammed its way into Rachel's consciousness.

"Are you okay, Rachel?" Shane asked.

No, I'm clearly going insane if I'm worrying about other women coveting my employer, she thought. *My employer. My employer. Nothing more, Everly. You don't want a man. Any man. Especially not a man with as much potential heartbreak written into his DNA as Shane Merritt. Remember that.*

"Rachel?"

"I'm sorry. I'm fine," she said. "Just planning out my afternoon." Which wasn't a lie, because this afternoon her plan was to completely stop thinking of Shane as a man and think of him only as her boss. Or, better yet, not at all.

CHAPTER FOUR

RACHEL was down on her knees with a bucket of soapy water and a sponge trying to put her "don't think about Shane" plan into action. She was trying not to think about how her entire body had gone hot and steamy when Shane had tucked his fingers beneath her chin yesterday. She was trying to pretend that an almost painful glow of gratitude hadn't warmed her heart when he'd been so understanding about her lack of domestic skills. The thing was…she wanted to trust him.

The other thing was…she didn't trust her own judgment. She'd been known to trust the wrong people, Dennis being the latest example, so wanting to trust Shane would be super-dumb. Shane had a bad reputation.

She scrubbed harder at a worn bit of linoleum. She put her back into it.

"That must be some stain," a feminine voice said.

Rachel turned to see a curly-haired woman standing in the doorway, holding two young children by the hands.

Rachel got to her feet and stepped forward. "Can I help you with something?"

The woman smiled and laughed. "I think it's supposed to be the other way around. If you're Rachel,

Shane sent me to help you. I'm Marcia. My husband, Hank, is going to be working for Shane the next few weeks. We've been living with Hank's parents in the next county, and they're wonderful, but the space is tight. The fact that Shane's lending us a cabin on the edge of his property will be a vacation for all of us."

"I'm glad to meet you, Marcia," Rachel said, returning the smile. It was, after all, impossible not to smile at the woman. She looked happy to be here. And when Marcia looked down at the little boy by her side and told him that he needed to not interrupt when people were speaking she said it gently and with obvious love in her voice.

Still, Rachel retraced her thoughts to the other woman's earlier comment. "Shane sent you to help me?"

Because he clearly didn't think she could handle things by herself.

"Just for today," Marcia said. "While you and I both get settled and he makes sure the cabin is ready. He'd planned for a single man, and he wants to add some safety features now that children will be staying there. These, by the way, are my children, Ella and Henry. They're both four."

And both adorable, she might as well have said. Ella had huge blue eyes that seemed to take everything in all at once, and Henry had the cutest little cowlick, which was just about all of him Rachel could see right now. Now that Rachel had moved forward, he was hiding behind his mother's leg.

"It's so nice to meet you, Ella and Henry. If your mom is going to be nice enough to lend me a hand, we'd better find something interesting for you to do. I'm pretty sure I saw some blocks around here somewhere."

Marcia blinked. "I'm new to the area, but when Hank got the call this morning I asked him about Oak Valley and...you have toys? I didn't know there were any children here."

"There aren't," Rachel said, just as if she knew a lot about this ranch. "And they're not exactly regular building blocks. More like sanded down pieces of wood. Maybe from when Shane was growing up. I've been told he was good at mathematical things, making things, engineering things. But no one's using them now. Would it be all right if Ella and Henry played with them? After you've checked them over, of course. I don't have much experience with children, so I'd want to make sure they passed the Mom safety test."

"I would love that," Marcia said. "We had to throw things together in a hurry and already I've lost track of which box I threw the toys in. Not to mention that other people's toys are always more interesting than what you have at home."

Rachel pulled out the box she'd found in a cabinet, revealing its contents. The pieces inside really did look like building blocks, but very unusual ones. They were carved in intricate shapes that locked together, the wood polished smooth.

"They're beautiful," Marcia said. "Maybe Shane won't want the kids to touch them."

Rachel considered that. "No. Shane has told me that he's selling everything here, lock, stock and barrel. He hasn't forbidden me to use anything." Except she wasn't to enter Eric's room. But that bit of information wasn't for sharing, not even with someone as nice as Marcia.

Within minutes, the two little cherubs were playing with the blocks of wood. Ella looked up at Rachel with excited eyes, and Henry's little body was wiggling with excitement. "We got goats," he said.

Rachel must have looked confused, because Marcia smiled. "Henry must really like you. We have a Nigerian dwarf goat, only one, and she's his pride and joy, a present for them being so good when we dragged them across the country. He's very possessive, so the fact that he would even share this bit of information with you is surprising."

"That's so exciting, Henry. I've seen some pictures of goats like that. They're awesome," Rachel said.

"Tunia," Ella explained.

"Ah, your goat's name is Petunia. I see."

Ella's smile lit up her whole little face.

"You got it," Marcia said with a laugh. "Most people don't understand little-people talk and want to know what kind of name Tunia is."

"It's a great name. I really like it," Rachel insisted, and Henry, who was trying to connect two pieces of wood, paused to show her his approval with a tiny smile that made her heart flip. Given the fact that she had decided she wasn't ever going to repeat her parents' horrific mistakes and marry, she would never have an Ella or Henry of her own, so moments like this were rare gifts.

"So, let me help you with this house," Marcia offered, and Rachel gratefully accepted.

The two women dove into work, Rachel peppering Marcia with questions and mentally recording the answers. By the time Shane showed up to announce that the cabin was now child-safe and Marcia could put the children down for a nap without worrying that they could get into anything dangerous when they got out of bed, the kitchen and dining rooms were both gleaming.

Even if there was still a lot that needed repairing and dressing up in both of those areas.

Rachel thanked Marcia and knelt down to whisper in both Ella and Henry's ears. "All right?" she finished.

Both of them nodded.

"Because, you know, this is Shane's ranch, and Petunia is going to love it here, so I think we should tell him that he's very lucky to be the landlord of someone as special as Petunia."

"Ella, Henry? You have another sister?" Shane asked, widening his eyes and dropping down to one knee, making himself less big and man-scary. Rachel remembered being very afraid of tall men when she was as young as these two.

Ella giggled. Henry shook his head emphatically. "Goat," he said.

"Goat," Ella echoed. "Tunia."

"Ah, I see," Shane said. "Well, then, I'm honored that you would bring Petunia to my ranch. I hope she—and you—like it here."

"Box," Henry said, making all of the adults frown with concentration.

But Rachel's mind was flipping through all the possibilities. "Did you like playing with Shane's blocks?"

Henry nodded emphatically, but Rachel saw that Shane was looking at the box of blocks as if he'd seen a ghost. "I thought those were long gone," he said.

Marcia and Rachel exchanged a look. Had she been wrong to let the children play with them? Had they—?

"I…thought I'd misplaced those. I'm glad you had fun with them," Shane said to Henry.

Not long after that, everyone said their goodbyes. Soon Rachel was alone with Shane.

"That was a good save," she told Shane. "Were the

blocks supposed to be off-limits? Were they…your brother's? I'm sorry. I should have asked if it was all right for the children to use them."

"No. You were right. It's scary for kids that young to come to a new place. I'm glad you pulled out the blocks."

"They look handmade."

He stared directly into her eyes. "A guy has to have something do to with his hands when he's closed up inside in the winter."

Which led Rachel to look down at Shane's big strong hands. She swallowed hard. She tried not to imagine those hands on her body.

"How old were you when you made them?"

"Twelve."

"Twelve? Only twelve?"

He shrugged. "It began because I'd broken the law. I took the principal's car for a joyride."

"At twelve," she said, more shocked than she wanted to let on.

"I was an unpleasant boy," he admitted. "Anyway, despite everyone in town thinking he was crazy, he agreed not to press charges and instead put me to work helping do odd jobs at the school. He saw my fascination with the woodworking tools for the shop class, and when my punishment was over, he showed me how to use them even though they were usually reserved for older students. The blocks you saw were more a learning process than anything."

She nodded. "I know some people might think that that was a light sentence, but your principal sounds like a wise man."

"He was. He's long gone, but he was the best man I ever knew."

Which must say something about Shane's relationship with his stepfather. But that was none of her business, was it? Because she and Shane weren't friends. He was her boss. And only her boss.

"I hope you'll be happy to hear that Marcia helped me make some food that won't kill you. At least not too quickly. I'll be home before you start to feel the effects," she said, trying for a lighter tone to slam herself back into the role of employee.

He chuckled, the serious look in his eyes fading away. "You're pretty saucy for a cook."

"Oh, I'm more than a cook," she said, heading for the stove. "With Marcia's and the internet's help, I now know how to clean a floor that you can lie down on wearing a white suit. This morning I was nothing. Tonight I am a woman with housecleaning superpowers. Or…at least I know enough about housecleaning to make sure you won't die of dirt poisoning."

She stopped and whirled around to face him and found that he had been walking behind her. He had been right on her heels, and now they were almost toe to toe. When she tipped her head up, his mouth was only inches above hers. His blue eyes were doing that wonderful smoldering thing that made her tingle.

He reached down as if to place his palms on her biceps, then dropped his arms to his sides. "Don't make me like you too much, Rachel. I don't want to do something we'll both regret."

Her heart was beating like some wild, out-of-control drum. She could barely breathe. "I don't want to do anything I'll regret, either," she whispered.

He groaned. He reached out and touched her hair, smoothing back a strand that had crept out of the ponytail she'd been wearing while she worked. Just that one barely-there caress sent shock waves through her entire body and nearly sent her over the edge. She bit back a moan, closed her eyes. She placed one hand on his chest, and she had no clue whether she was trying to push herself away from him or whether she simply had to feel his heart pounding beneath her palm.

But he must have assumed the first. "Open your eyes, Rachel," he whispered, taking a big step away. Cool air slipped over her now empty palm. "I'm not going to touch you. I know you have serious trust issues. You know I have issues, too. One of them being the fact that I'm going to be gone in less than three weeks, and nothing is going to stop me from going. This project has to be done—this house will be sold even if I have to drop the price to nothing. And once I leave Moraine I'm never coming back."

"Me, either," she whispered. Even though she suspected that he was running away from an old life and she was trying to run to a new one. Either way, they were just together now on a very temporary pass.

She took a step back herself. "We should eat," she said.

So they sat. They ate.

"It's good," Shane told her.

It wasn't, but it wasn't horrible. And anyway, she mused, after she had returned to Ruby's, after the initial taste she hadn't registered a single bite she'd taken. Because she'd realized how close she'd come today to crossing a line that couldn't be crossed.

Despite years of avoiding the kind of relationship that had made her life a misery, she had wanted Shane to touch her. She had craved the taste of his lips so intensely that it was a miracle she hadn't shoved him down and had her kissing way with him.

Only Shane's resolve had saved her. Because if he hadn't backed off…well, she had the worst feeling that he could have told her anything, asked for anything, and despite the fact that she didn't actually trust him— and she knew for sure that he could and would hurt her—she might have given him much more than she could recover from.

Instead, he'd backed away. He hadn't kissed her. She should be drowning in buckets of relief right now. She should be thanking the stars that she had been saved from her own stupid desires.

If only she could stop wondering what it would have been like if they had a redo and this time their lips actually touched.

In the middle of the night, two days later, Rachel had an epiphany. "Decorating," she told Shane when she got out of the car and approached him the next morning. "You need decorating. Clean up, fix up, renovate up, decorate up. The ranchers will come for the ranch, I assume, but they have to live in the house. There's no life in the house. We have to change that."

Shane had been drinking coffee, leaning against the porch support, his ankles crossed as he slouched in that casual cowboy pose and surveyed the horizons of the ranch. The sun had risen but it was still a pink and gold ball reaching fingers of rose up to the sky. He turned to Rachel now as if she'd just suggested that he buy an elephant and put it on the porch.

"Slow down, Rachel. Back up. Why do we need to blow up the house?"

She gave him the evil eye. "You know what I mean. You said that you'd sell the house at any price, because you couldn't stay, but that seems such a shame. While

Marcia and I were cleaning, I scrubbed down to golden woodwork. There are some nice light fixtures underneath the grease that's built up. The place could look a lot better and it would sell faster if it just…looked a little nicer."

He was staring at her intently. "You're not getting too wrapped into this, are you?"

She started to say no. It was what he wanted to hear and what she wanted to say. "Maybe a little. I have a bad habit of jumping in with both feet. It goes…way back. It's gotten me in trouble on more than one occasion. I won't bore you with the details, but you're right. I'll try to slow down. But will you mind if I at least do a little with the place?"

"I don't mind. If you enjoy doing it, I have no objection at all. I just don't want things to get too complicated. I'm trying to keep my repairs to the minimum. This is more of a 'think of the possibilities' sale. I don't want to c— I don't want to spend too much time on it."

For a second there she'd thought he had been going to say that he didn't want to care. Maybe he had. That implied that he had feelings about this place, that there was a history here he wasn't ready to give up. There was, Rachel admitted, a lot she didn't know about Shane. He was a man with shadows in his life, a man with a patchy history. It was better not to know too much about him, she was sure. As he had started to say, it was better not to care.

"I'll be very blasé as I improve the ranch," she promised him, tilting up her chin and tossing her hair back.

"Somehow I don't think the word blasé has ever been used where you're concerned," he said. "I bow to your decorating expertise, Rachel. I'm sure there'll be a few people who will be just as interested in the house as the ranch itself."

"Maybe more than a few," she said, looking off to the side.

He stepped to the side so that he was looking into her eyes. "Care to clarify?"

"I might have mentioned the open house to Ruby and Angie. They might have told a few people. I think there may be a large contingent of Moraine women showing up on that day. You know. Just to look."

He swore beneath his breath.

"I know. I know. You don't like Moraine."

"It's more complicated than that." But he didn't elaborate.

"I'm sorry," she said. "But if the women come… they have friends and family and associates elsewhere. Even if they don't buy, they may know someone who might. And they'll have cameras and phones. Word will spread."

His face looked stony and…something else. There was that look in his eyes she could never quite decipher. As if ghosts lived in his eyes. And because she was standing so close, watching so carefully, she noted the moment when he closed off those ghost thoughts and gave in to the inevitable.

"I suppose you're right. And it's just one day. I can manage one day if in the end I achieve my goal."

Yes! she wanted to say. She had told her secret and he hadn't fired her. She had given him news she knew he would hate and he apparently didn't hate her yet. But she said nothing, because even though he had conceded her point, it was still obvious that he didn't like it. Gloating was not allowed.

"I'll give you a free hand with the house," he said,

"but for today can you spare me an hour or two? I need you to come with me, to document a few things with your camera."

"Not a problem," she said casually, although excitement was already bubbling up inside her. She hadn't taken a single photo in days. That was the only reason she was so eager. Wasn't it? It had nothing to do with the fact that she would be spending time with Shane.

Behave yourself, she warned herself. *Try not to act like some teenage nerd who just snagged a date with the prom king.* She hated, hated, hated that kind of thing. Still, her feet tripped along faster as she picked up her camera and returned to where Shane was standing.

"Today we ride," he told her.

Okay, so maybe there *was* a problem.

CHAPTER FIVE

"You need boots for riding," Shane mused as he walked with Rachel over to the corral, where Hank was seeing to the horses that had arrived a bit later than expected. "Those shoes are too slippery."

"No, I'm okay. I'm not...I'm not riding," Rachel said, her voice sounding slightly strained. Shane couldn't help glancing down at her. Was she looking a little pale?

"Rachel? Everything all right?"

"Everything's fine. Just great. Shane, your horses are so amazing. They're beautiful," she said, just as if everything was, indeed, all right. But something was slightly off here. Shane blinked at that. He'd only known the woman a few days. Why was he having thoughts like that? How would he know when something was right or wrong with Rachel? Why would he care?

In some ways, everything seemed perfectly normal. She had opened the case on her camera and was lining up a shot already, but when she'd finished taking the picture she didn't move closer to the horses.

He approached the fence, whickered softly, and a pretty chestnut mare tossed her head lightly and moved up to him. "Rachel, this is Lizzie. She's very gentle." He held his hand out and Lizzie nudged up against him.

"She knows you," Rachel said.

"Well, I don't know if she still does. We haven't seen each other in a long while. But Lizzie was always a friendly horse. You can touch her if you like. She'll stand still for you."

When he looked at Rachel, her brown eyes were glowing. "I've never touched a horse before." But she looked eager enough. And even though she approached Lizzie tentatively, she did manage to make contact.

Lizzie pressed up against Rachel's palm.

"Oh, you are a sweetheart," Rachel said.

By now Hank and Tom, another new hand, had brought a couple of the other horses over. "This one's a stranger to me," Shane said. "And this is Rambler." Rambler was a big, spirited bay.

"If you've been gone ten years, your horses must have been very young when you left," Rachel said, her voice soft and tentative.

"Some of them like Lizzie, yes. Some died during that time and others were born. The horses are my one regret about leaving the ranch, but my lifestyle doesn't allow for pets. I should have sold them already."

"Leaving…things behind is difficult."

He glanced at her. Her voice had dropped. She looked pensive, a little sad, but then she shook her head and looked up at him.

"Are you going to sell them with Oak Valley?"

"I'm not sure. They're more window dressing right now. Setting the stage."

"Actors?" she suggested. "Lizzie looks like she'd like to be a star."

He chuckled. "She's a show off and yes, she's a star. Now—" he hesitated "—are you ready to ride?"

Rachel took a full step back. As if he'd just suggested that she wear a python for a necklace. "I—no. I'm sorry, but I'm not going to do that."

She was fidgeting in a way he'd never seen before, her fingers twisting up against each other.

As if she'd just realized what she'd said, her eyes opened wide. She looked horrified. "Maybe I should rephrase that," she began.

He shook his head. "Shh, it's okay. Just take your photos and then I'll drive you to the other sites."

"I'm sorry," she said.

"No need to be."

"You said that it was difficult to get to those other places with a car."

"I'll dig out the ATVs. Ever ride one?"

"No."

"Are you okay with trying it?"

"Totally fine with it."

Which sounded much more Rachel-like. She had already volunteered to learn how to drive a stick shift and change the oil and spark plugs in a car without a second glance. She'd been uncomfortable with cooking and cleaning, but in spite of that she'd tackled those tasks without flinching. And clearly she was enchanted with Lizzie and the horses, just not with riding one. Shane couldn't help wondering what had happened to her.

He scowled. From the beginning he'd known it wasn't wise to get too close to Rachel. That hadn't changed. In fact it had been more than obvious when he had been on the verge of giving her a full-on kiss the other day. He should just drop the horse issue.

Yeah, he really should do that. What difference did it make that Rachel would go through life without experiencing the joy of riding a horse? Not everyone in the world had to know that kind of pleasure.

"Why are you frowning at me?" she asked.

Shane blinked. "I wasn't frowning at you. Just thinking ahead to something I need to do, a problem I need to work out. Let's go find that ATV. I've got one with a rack for your equipment."

A short time later they were racing across the fields on ATVs, Rachel's dark mane flowing out behind her.

Shane stopped to show her the field where they were making hay. As the mower cut through the field, Rachel breathed in deeply of the cut grasses.

"It smells wonderful," she said. "What happens to it next? You just scoop it up into one of those hay baler things?"

"Eventually we bundle it up with the baler. But first we have to make sure that the moisture content is right, so once it's cut we leave it in windrows to dry. Then it's raked to help with the drying, and finally it's baled and stored until it's needed for the animals in winter."

"That's…nice."

He looked at her.

"No. I mean it. There must be something very satisfying about growing the feed for your animals all by yourself."

He tilted his head. "I grew up like this. Hadn't given it much thought. I never was much of a rancher."

"But you know how to do that?" She pointed toward the mower.

Shane shrugged. "I started this morning at first light and then turned things over to Tom when I went up to the house."

"Because you had to meet me?"

"Because you and I had things to do." But he couldn't deny that he'd felt a sense of anticipation waiting for Rachel to arrive. "Come on. Do you have some shots we might use?"

"I think so. Where to next?"

She was like a kid at a five-star amusement park. He led her around the ranch to a cabin meant as a winter shelter, and she entered the place as if it was some sort of treasure cave.

"I can imagine some pioneer woman cooking soup over a fire here, making candles, fighting the elements."

He couldn't help smiling. "I don't think it's quite that old, but, yes, the basic original idea was to protect a rider from the elements if he should get caught on the far side of the ranch. Not sure this one was ever used for anything more than a getaway."

She stopped to marvel at a field of yellow balsamroot and blue lupines. "I've never seen so many flowers in one place. There must be thousands of them." There were, but although he'd appreciated their beauty in the past, he'd never thought of them as anything special. They bloomed every year. On the ranch, they became just some pretty flowers he passed as he went about his chores.

"Let's move on," he said, not wanting to analyze his reaction too closely. It didn't matter, anyway. Soon the ranch would belong to someone else.

They made their way past grazing land, over hills and into valleys, until he stopped beside a clear, cold creek tumbling over rocks.

Rachel knelt and picked up a flat stone. "What a pretty pink! May I? Ranch souvenir?" she asked.

He laughed. "Be my guest. But it won't look nearly as nice once it dries."

"You sound so…adult," she said with a laugh. "But I'll bet you and…I'll bet you collected your share in your day." A guilty look came over Rachel's face at her stumble.

She was right. He and his brother had filled their pockets with stones, Eric always sure that the next stone would still be bright once it dried.

The familiar and still fresh pain flowed through Shane, but he wasn't going to have Rachel feeling guilty just for making a casual comment. Guilt was a cruel master, as he well knew.

"I ripped the pockets of plenty of jeans with the weight of those rocks. I used to camp by this stream in summer," he said. No need to mention that on one or two of those occasions it was because he'd run away from home.

"That sounds very romantic. The cowboy, his horse and a campfire beside a stream. The stuff that entices people to read Westerns and dream of coming to places like this."

It had never been that way for him. He'd been on the run…until duty had called him home. "Hey, I thought you were a Maine girl."

She smiled. "I am. I will be. But even a Maine girl isn't immune to the lure of a campfire under the western stars."

"I could see you here," he said suddenly. Because it was true. In a world gone dark, under a sky full of stars stretching from horizon to horizon, he could imagine Rachel looking up with those brown eyes that filled with wonder whenever she witnessed something new or exciting.

"Am I wearing a cowgirl hat and boots in your imagination?" she teased. "You told me today that I needed boots."

"I hadn't gotten that far," he admitted. "I wasn't imagining clothing." Although now that she'd brought it up and now that he'd said it in that ill-conceived way, he was definitely imagining her without clothes, wrapped up in a blanket with him. He wanted to groan.

"What were you imagining?" she asked, stepping closer.

"It's probably better not to say," he told her.

And there it was. The blush.

"I've never met a woman who blushes the way you do," he said. And then, as if he didn't have an ounce of sense in his head, he slid one hand beneath her hair and kissed her cheek, where the rose-pink blush had taken up residence. He tracked it down, kissing the delicate line of her jaw, her neck, where he could feel her pulse fluttering.

She was clutching his shoulders, trembling beneath his hands, and for a moment he forgot all reason. He touched his lips to hers, and his senses exploded. She was honey and cinnamon, woman and sunlight. He wanted more of her. Much more. Now. This second.

Rachel leaned into him when the kiss ended. She returned the kiss and the heat climbed. But soon he felt her hands against his chest. "I shouldn't be doing this," she said. "I shouldn't, because…because…"

She didn't have to explain. And she was right. So very right. He released her immediately. "Because you're a girl from Maine and I'm a man on his way out of Montana."

"And you're my boss and I'm your housekeeper.

And because I promised myself that this wouldn't happen," she said.

And so had he. He was a man who never made promises. This was just another reason why. "I apologize for stepping over the line."

Rachel shook her head. "I knew what I was doing. I'd been warned. Numerous times. I'd told myself not to do something like this. More than once. You might have kissed first, but I kissed last."

What could he say to that? She'd been warned about him, and with good reason. And now he had broken her trust. He wanted to tell her that it wouldn't happen again, but he no longer trusted himself. "I'd better get you back to the house" was the best that he could do.

She sighed. "I'm sorry this messed up the workday. I don't think you meant to finish this soon."

Finally he found a reason to smile. "Rachel, if you think this messed up the workday…there are millions of men who wish their workdays could end like this." But he *was* sorry. She'd been enjoying the day and now she wasn't. There was no way to fix that. The only good thing was that now he knew just how risky being close to Rachel was. He needed to be more careful. He needed to work faster. It was more important than ever that he finish with Oak Valley quickly. Maybe he should try to speed up the process.

Rachel felt as if twin storms were having a battle inside her chest the next morning. Shane had kissed her…and she had kissed him back.

What was I thinking? The question ran through her mind in a continuous loop. But why even ask that question, anyway? Because she hadn't been thinking. She'd just been feeling, reacting in that whole mindless man-

woman way that had never worked out in her family.
She'd sworn she would never let go that way. And she
never had.

But, darn it, the man could kiss.

"Grr," she said beneath her breath.

"Rachel? Everything okay? You need help?" Shane's
voice came from outside and Rachel jumped, banging
her knee into the corner of a cabinet and biting back
the pain to keep from yelling.

"No, I'm fine," she said quickly. "What are you
doing out there?"

She got her answer when he came inside carrying
a ladder. "I was just on my way to repair the molding
around the window in the dining room and…why is
your knee bleeding?"

Rachel looked down, and sure enough there was a
thin trickle of blood seeping from a small cut, tracing
a path down toward her sandal. The edge of the cabinet
had been sharp, but she hadn't noticed the cut. She'd
been so intent on avoiding contact with Shane. Now
that they'd been intimate—or as close to intimate as
they were ever going to get—she felt awkward in his
presence.

"It's nothing," she said as casually as possible. "Go
fix your molding. I'll just wash it off."

He frowned. "It's not nothing. It could get infected.
Infection is dangerous. Sit down. We're taking care of
this right now."

He was going to touch her? Touch her knee? With
those big hands that had been touching her in her
dreams last night? When both of them had been naked?
She cursed her decision to wear shorts today. If she'd
been wearing jeans, none of this would be happening.

"No, really, I can do it," she began.

"Rachel, stop it. I'm not going to do anything inti-mate." There was that word again. "I'm just going to make sure you're okay. You're on my watch right now. I can't have you getting injured. I've seen…I know what can happen if a person doesn't take care of something small and it becomes major. All right?"

She nodded slowly. Because while his words were asking permission, those stormy eyes of his told her that she didn't have a choice.

Rachel sat. Shane disappeared for a few minutes and returned with a first aid kit. He washed his hands, then pulled up a stool in front of Rachel. He took a cloth he had dampened, leaned forward and gently dabbed away the blood.

She tried to keep breathing normally. So far there was cloth between his skin and hers. "Um, how is your work going?" she asked, trying to appear nonchalant.

A trace of a smile appeared on his lips as he contin-ued to work. Had he noticed the tremor in her voice?

"Got a lot done. The barn is finished, I have a small crew on fences. There's still a lot to do. Repair work on at least one of the tractors, some major windmill issues, other outbuildings that need work and some dead trees that need to be removed. But we might finish up sooner than later."

"Sooner?" So she had less time than she had thought. For some reason a sense of sadness pulsed through her. Probably just because she wasn't nearly as far along as he was, she told herself. It had nothing to do with the fact that she and Shane would be finishing their time together sooner. After all, her whole life had been about leaving places. She was good at it.

"I'd better pick up the pace, too. I've done at least the surface cleaning of all of the rooms. That is, I mean, most of the rooms." She faltered and took a breath. Why had she said that? It was just…Shane was touching her and she wasn't thinking clearly. And, okay, yes, she couldn't help worrying about the fact that Shane was clearly still in pain if he couldn't face his brother's belongings yet, and she—darn it, she'd always been a fixer type of person. Or at least she'd tried to fix the unfixable.

"I can work faster." She ended in a whoosh.

Shane paused. "Rachel."

"I'm sorry. I shouldn't have even mentioned it. Not the working faster. The other."

"I know what you meant," he said, his blue eyes dark, masking his thoughts. "I don't want you to worry about it. When the time comes I'll handle it, but…not yet."

She nodded tightly.

"I don't want you to be uncomfortable."

"I won't be. I'm not." Which was such a total lie. With Shane's hands still on her they were kissing close, even if no kissing was going on. And she was worried about him.

"Don't worry about the room."

"No. I won't."

He looked unconvinced. She didn't want to give him anything else to worry about. "I've got plenty to keep me busy. All that decorating to do," she said. "And if we're finishing sooner than expected, I'd better start thinking about where I go from here." She did her best to inject some cheer into her voice. "Maine's a big place."

Shane was looking down. He had resumed cleaning her cut, but now his hand stalled in his task. He had moved from the cloth to a much smaller disinfectant pad. His fourth and fifth fingers rested on her knee. He pinned her with his gaze. Rachel tried to keep breathing.

"You're telling me that when you leave here you have no specific place to go?"

"Well, I have a general area. But not one place, no. I should start looking."

"And how are you going to do that?" he asked, a bit too carefully, as he took a bandage out of a box and began to ready it.

Breathe. Breathe. Breathe, Rachel ordered herself. "I'll just do a general internet search. There are places where people list their apartments and you just contact them."

"Might not be safe." He gently smoothed the bandage into place, turning every nerve in her body to the *on* position. "You should only contact people you know you can trust."

What should she say to that? Not that there was no one she trusted that much, or that there was no one she would allow to help her with this important a decision. "Well, it's been a while since I was there last."

His hands were both resting on her leg now. He was staring into her eyes. "I know people in the business. They're very good at what they do. Let me put you in touch with them."

And now, with his hands against her, his voice rumbled through her body. She slugged in a deep breath, nodded fiercely. "All right. Yes. Thank you." Anything to end this before she leaned forward, grabbed his lapels, yanked him to her and repeated yesterday's kiss.

As if he knew what she was thinking, he released her. He stood. "Tonight," he promised. "If you don't mind staying a little later than usual?"

Oh, no. Ruby was going to have a field day with this, she thought, followed immediately by her own admonitions.

Stop worrying about Ruby. You just behave yourself. No more thinking about kissing Shane. Not unless you actually want your heart broken so badly that you'll never recover.

Not a chance. Ever.

"Tonight will be fine," she agreed.

No problem at all. She could handle anything.

Rachel tiptoed into the inn. Ruby always left the kitchen light on in case a guest needed a glass of water in the middle of the night. Pale light filtered out of the kitchen into the neighboring rooms, so Rachel had no trouble seeing her way through the house.

She breathed a sigh of relief that Ruby had already gone to bed. There would be no questions about what she'd been doing hanging around with Shane after dark.

And if Ruby was asleep she wouldn't be up until the next morning. Rachel's landlady slept the sleep of the contented. Nothing disturbed her once she was down for the night.

Slipping her shoes off and padding toward the staircase, Rachel was nearly to the first step when Ruby's voice stopped her. "Good, you're home. You were out pretty late tonight, weren't you, hon?"

Rachel turned. She was surprised to hear genuine worry in her landlady's voice. She wasn't used to anyone caring when she came home and guilt slipped through her. Dropping to the steps, she sat down. "I'm sorry I didn't let you know I wasn't coming back to the inn at my usual time. But it's only nine-thirty. I thought you were asleep."

"At nine-thirty?"

"Ruby, you just implied that it was late," Rachel pointed out with an exasperated smile.

"For young women cavorting with men who radiate testosterone. Not for old ladies waiting to hear what happened."

Uh-oh. There was too much interest in Ruby's voice. Rachel reminded herself that in Moraine nothing much happened. Little incidents made bigger splashes than they would in a larger town. Even when those little splashes didn't mean a thing.

"*Nothing* happened," she told her friend. "Shane was just helping me look for a place to stay when I get to Maine." And in truth, that was all that had happened. They had circled each other carefully at first, but eventually Shane had pulled up two chairs in front of the computer, brought out two glasses of wine, and they had discussed the pros and cons of different areas of Maine. He'd been there often in the past, even though his business hadn't taken him to that part of the country in recent years.

"So you like the tang of the salt air, the rocky coasts and picturesque little Cape Cod houses? Lobster traps and lighthouses?" he'd asked.

She'd laughed. "You say that as if it's a bad thing."

"Not at all. It's a beautiful part of the country. Any reason why Maine is your choice?"

Rachel had run her thumb over the stem of the wine glass. "I spent several years there growing up. It was the best time of my life."

He'd tilted his head in acquiescence. "Then Maine it is."

After that, they'd moved on to specific areas and he'd pulled out some ideas a former colleague had emailed him earlier in the day. By the time she'd gone home, Rachel had had a much better idea of where she might like to move and put down roots. That should have been one of the brightest moments in the past few weeks, but for now…

Something very close to sadness rippled through her. She felt as if she'd crossed something off on a list of things to do, but there was no satisfaction in the accomplishment. It was probably just because she was tired. Tomorrow the anticipation would finally kick in.

"Hello? Rachel?" Ruby snapped her fingers and Rachel opened her eyes wide.

"Sorry. I was just thinking about a house."

"Yeah."

"What?"

"You spent the night sitting knee to knee with Shane and all you can think about is a house? Rachel, I'm twenty years too old for the man, but if I'd been closed up with him after dark my mind wouldn't have been on houses."

"It's not like that with us," Rachel protested. Except when it was.

"Okay, I'll stop pestering you. When are we going to get to see him again?"

"You want me to bring him here?"

Ruby grinned. "Hon, I'd like nothing better, but I was talking about convincing him to come back to town. The man has been here for a week but he's barely touched foot in Moraine and he'll be leaving soon. People would like to see him. He grew up here. He's Moraine family to us."

Uh-oh. If there was one thing Rachel knew, it was

that Shane didn't want to go to Moraine. She didn't know why, but she knew it was so.

"He's really busy and…I'm not a miracle worker, Ruby."

"You're a woman. Use your wiles."

Rachel should have laughed at that, but the truth was that it occurred to her at that moment that the only reason Shane was kissing her was because there were no other single women around. But there had to be single women in Moraine…which he was avoiding.

"Ruby, why do you think a man like Shane wouldn't want to go back to his hometown? What happened here? What did people do to him?"

Ruby shook her head. "I don't know. I know that Shane lost his mother at a young age, that he and Frank didn't get along and that Eric died in a ranch accident. But there's nothing anyone in town did or said to him that I can think of. Not a thing. But, believe it or not, I don't know everything. Maybe you should ask Shane. And if you can't get him there by using your wiles, maybe remind him that those are his potential customers."

That was a hoot. Wiles again? Rachel had none. Never had, never would. And she didn't want them. Wiles never got you anything good…or lasting.

But she did think that Ruby had a point about Shane going to town to meet his customers. If he really wanted to sell Oak Valley quickly—and he had made it clear that he did—and if he was a good businessman—and he apparently was—then why wasn't he using his networking skills with the people who might help him spread the word and sell the ranch?

Rachel didn't have a clue. Maybe Shane wasn't thinking clearly because he was still mourning Eric.

Maybe she should just mind her own business, stay out of things, keep quiet.

But she'd never been especially good at any of those things. Besides, Shane had stepped over a personal line when he'd opted to help her find a place in Maine. He was helping her. What kind of a person would she be if she didn't try her best to help him, too?

CHAPTER SIX

SHANE woke up the next morning the way he always did. Early. He headed for the bathroom to take a shower and shave the way he always did. He ignored the closed door of Eric's room, trying to pretend he wasn't going to have to open it soon and let the past beat him up for a failure he should have foreseen and a loss he could never get over. The truth was that he'd been running all his life, but now he had to run faster to stay ahead of his demons. The other truth was that he couldn't put off opening that room forever. Rachel was starting to worry.

He told himself he didn't care. His problems were his and only his, as they had always been.

That seemed to help. For about two seconds. Before he remembered just how difficult it was to look into her brown eyes and feel as if he was failing her.

He hated failing people. For some reason it was worse with her. Maybe because she was sunny most of the time.

Too bad, he told himself. It couldn't matter. It *didn't* matter. Because he knew what would happen once he started sifting through Eric's possessions.

Shane closed his eyes. He took a few deep breaths. Finally he convinced himself that it was all right to put the inevitable off for one more day, and he stepped into the shower and let the hot water melt the kinks he'd accumulated from the hard physical labor of the day before.

All right, he was in control of himself now. The day would be just fine. He had it all planned out. He was ready to get dressed, have coffee and hit the ground running, maybe do some repairs on the calving shed, pound some boards to take the edge off.

Then, when he was good and worn out, he would have lunch with Rachel, eat some of that stuff she was trying so hard to make edible.

He smiled at the thought. They'd talk, he'd sneak a few questions in about her plans for the future—why had he thought she had it all planned out? How had he not known she didn't even have a place to go?

But now he knew and he intended to help. Then he'd maybe sneak in a little time with her and the horses, get Lizzie to love her up a little more. Stupid idea. What difference did it make if she was afraid of getting on a horse? And why was it bothering him so much?

It's not, he told himself. Still…they'd have a go at Lizzie again. Yeah, that was the plan. Easy. Nothing too stressful. No tension.

He climbed from the shower, wrapped a towel around himself and stepped out into the hallway.

Right into Rachel's path.

She froze in her tracks. Her gaze took in the rivulets of water tracking down his chest.

"I-it's early, I know," she said hastily. "But I—the house. I wanted to talk to you about something. I wanted to catch you before you got busy."

He wasn't busy now. He was…fascinated by the way her eyes slid away from him, then returned, never rising to meet his gaze. But he was also aware that he was making her uncomfortable.

"Just let me get dressed and I'll be right with you."

Rachel gave a quick nod. "Okay, I'll…make some coffee, start some breakfast."

He wanted to smile at that. She hadn't cooked breakfast for him before. He either had her really discombobulated or she wanted to ask him something she thought he might not like. Maybe some froufrou thing for the house. Heck, he didn't care what she put in the house. He had the money to pay for it and he wouldn't be looking at it much longer, anyway.

"That'd be nice, but you know, I don't require you to make my breakfast."

She lifted one delicious dark eyebrow. "Are you afraid of my breakfast, Shane?"

He crossed his arms over his chest. "Do I look like I'm afraid?" He raised an eyebrow, too. Two could play at that game.

And now she surprised him. She stared directly at him, her eyes resting on his muscles, playing chicken. Where had she learned that kind of fortitude when he knew that intimacy made her nervous?

"Well, I can at least make toast," she said. "And coffee."

But in the end it turned out that she couldn't. When he came into the kitchen she shoved a bowl, a box of cereal and some milk and orange juice in front of him. The scent of burnt toast hung in the air.

"I would have eaten it," he said. "It tastes better that way."

She wrinkled her nose at him. "No fair going easy on me just because you know I don't know what I'm doing."

"I'm not. Really. You're learning and you haven't complained about the challenges, even though ranching and housekeeping are outside your familiar comfort zone."

Shane meant every word; he'd meant them to be encouraging, but Rachel was looking as if he'd just shown her a video of a sad puppy.

He tried again. "Everyone should be given a chance to learn. No one should be criticized for not being an expert at everything. We all have our strong suits." He couldn't begin to explain how strongly he felt about that. It was his mantra.

"Thank you," she said. "But I'm still not feeding you burnt toast."

He smiled and she returned the smile. Thank goodness. "Now, what can I do for you?" he asked.

She ran one hand down the leg of her jeans, looking as if she was about to ask for the moon. "I want you to come to Moraine with me."

Not happening, he thought. "Why would you want me to do that?" he asked, his voice careful and emotionless.

"I told you that I want to do some redecorating. I think—as the owner—you should have some say in what colors I put on your walls and what kinds of curtains I hang."

He shook his head slowly. "I'm not really that involved in that kind of thing. Whatever you do will be fine."

To his surprise, Rachel took a step closer. She held out a hand as if she was going to touch him. "What if I painted the walls purple and put curtains with big red butterflies in your bedroom?"

He tilted his head. "Have a thing for red butterflies, do you?"

She frowned, and he could practically see the wheels turning in her head. "You can see that I don't have much practice with domestic affairs. My taste might not match yours."

But he glanced down at her blue jeans, her pale blue blouse and the delicate gold chain on her wrist. He reached out, took her hand and rubbed his thumb gently over the delicate skin near the bracelet. "I like this," he said. "It's not gaudy and you haven't shown any signs of extremism in anything you've worn. So… what's this about, Rachel?"

"I—" She gazed up into his eyes, her lips parted slightly, and he realized what a mistake he had made. He'd been trying to overpower her, to get her to open up and confess what her motivations were, because they clearly had nothing to do with purple paint. But now, with his thumb resting on the soft skin of her wrist and with that pretty mouth urging him to kiss it closed, he was the one who was discombobulated. "I— Ruby and some of the other people in Moraine want to have some time to spend with you before you leave. They're all hoping that you'll come to town soon."

Just like that, he dropped her hand, stood up and took a big step back. "That's not happening."

"I don't understand."

"I don't expect you to, Rachel. You weren't here with me when I lived here."

"Did people mistreat you?"

He blinked at that. "Rachel, you've met Ruby."

"Well, Ruby, yes. But she's special."

"She is. She's very special. And she never mistreated me. Neither did anyone else. Rachel, I can't explain it, but going to town brings back memories I have to forget. I don't like to talk about my past. The most I can say is that no one goes through life without leaving tracks wherever they go. I'm not retracing mine."

Rachel frowned. "If you're talking about what Ruby told me that first day, or the episode when you stole the car...I haven't heard anyone saying anything negative about you. Well, other than Ruby's comments about you being...you know. But Ruby didn't say that out of malice."

"I know. She said it because she was concerned for you. But...I don't intend to hurt you, Rachel. Neither do I intend to set foot in town."

Rachel opened her mouth to speak. Shane stepped forward and gently laid two fingers over her lips.

"No," he said. "Just no. Go to town, Rachel. Buy whatever you like for the house and charge it to me. But I won't be going. That's final."

Or so he thought. He started to step away and she placed her hand—very lightly—on his bare arm. Sensation sizzled through him. What was that about? They were having a discussion, a painful discussion, and even then the woman's touch affected him. He did his best to ignore it, because if there was one thing these past few moments had brought home to him it was how close he was coming to leaving yet another person damaged. It could happen so easily if he didn't watch himself. Rachel acted tough at times, but she was held together with visibly fragile threads and she was here alone. There was no one to watch out for her.

Except for him. Someone needed to watch her back. He intended to make sure she was protected, even if it was from himself. So he looked down at where her fingers lay against his skin, trying to reestablish the employer/employee relationship. She was usually so conscientious about that stuff. He was sure she would back off, and then he could erect some walls around himself...which would be the best thing for her.

To his surprise, she didn't let go, although she did look very self-conscious about touching him. "Shane, I think this is a mistake. Whatever you said or did... you should never leave a place without settling your debts and doing whatever you can to make sure that everyone is happy."

"Is that another of your teacher's 'one size fits all' lessons?"

Her color rose high, but she didn't back down. "No, it's all Rachel Everly. Just something I learned at a very early age."

He had no clue what she was saying, but he knew for certain that somehow someone had hurt Rachel. And it wasn't just that jerk Dennis. The look in her eyes told him that this was a very personal lesson.

So, despite his best intentions, he slid one hand beneath her hair and gently rubbed his thumb across her lips. "Rachel, that's what I'm trying to do. I'm trying to make sure that I leave everyone here as happy as is possible."

"But they want to see you. They want your company. That's...such a gift. It's so special. I would—"

The intensity in her voice and the fact that she couldn't continue...what was *that* about? Shane realized once again that Rachel hadn't shared any real information about her past, and—amazingly—he realized that he wanted to know, even though knowing more of Rachel probably wasn't wise.

Still, he wouldn't pry. He more than most understood the need for emotional walls. "What would you do?" he coaxed, releasing her.

She shook her head. "What I would do doesn't really matter, does it? I'm the impulsive one, the one who ended up stranded here with no money."

"Don't," he warned with a scowl. "Don't demean yourself. You have a 'forge ahead' attitude and a gift for finding joy in the small moments in life that most people lack. If we could bottle that...people would pay buckets of money for it. We could all use a little Rachel in our lives."

And there it was, that beautiful blush that revealed the innocence beneath her "I can be anything" exterior.

But as the blush faded she crossed her arms. "I see what you're doing. You're trying to turn all business-man, all salesman on me, so that I'll leap for the compliment and forget that we were talking about you."

He raised one eyebrow. "Was that what I was doing?"

"You know it was."

She was wrong. He hadn't been trying to trick her. He'd meant every word. But he knew why she would think that. Trust was a fragile element and her trust had been broken. Maybe more than once, judging from the things she was leaving unsaid.

"You're wrong. Believe me." But he knew that she wouldn't. And why should she? Everything she'd been told about him urged her not to trust. And everything she'd been told was absolutely true.

"It doesn't matter," she said. "What matters is that... Shane, you have neighbors who want to see you. They like you. Do you really want to turn away from that?"

And they were back to him, back to doors he had

locked and didn't want to open. "I'm doing what I need to do, Rachel."

This time he managed to walk away. And this time she didn't try to get him to stay.

"What's going on out there at the ranch? Looks like you and Shane are setting up house," the woman at the register said to Rachel. Her name tag said that she was Cynthia Corvellis. To Rachel she was *the enemy,* if she was going to start spreading rumors about Shane.

Rachel forced a stiff smile. The part of her that was smart and sensible knew that she should just leave the store now, but the other part of her that had never been able to back down from ugly situations was out in full force today. She knew why, too. It was because Shane had complimented her during their argument and—Jupiter and Juno—warmth had slipped through her. She'd wanted to believe him. Worse, she'd wanted to touch him.

All of that was wrong. Believing compliments had gotten her in trouble before. Forgetting that Shane was her boss and only her boss was going to end up in big, big, heart-killing trouble. And here was this woman implying that she and Shane were…were *doing it* when that was just never going to happen in this lifetime. Nothing was going to happen between her and Shane, ever, unless you counted her nearly killing him with her meals twice a day. Having this Cynthia person fishing for spicy gossip today…it just crossed a line.

Rachel leaned over the counter slightly. She lowered her voice. "What would you think if I told you yes? Shane and I are getting married."

Cynthia blinked. "For real? He's settling down? Here? With you?" Her tone made it clear that she would be less surprised to see aliens from some distant planet walking around town.

And yet, when a smile of pure pleasure slipped over the woman's face, all the spunk and nasty slipped right out of Rachel. What was wrong with her? Why would she say something like that to this total stranger? "No. I'm very sorry. I was just…I lied. I'm only Shane's housekeeper, and I'm just here to buy curtains for his house because the ones there look as if someone put them through a cheese-shredder."

To her surprise, Cynthia reached out and patted her on the shoulder. "I know why you lied. He's a real hard man to love, isn't he, hon?"

Rachel blinked. "I—I don't love Shane."

But it was obvious that Cynthia didn't believe her by the pitying look in her eyes. "I've done more than my share of comforting the girls Shane has left behind in my time. He never stays."

Wasn't that almost exactly what Ruby had told her? What was wrong with the women of Moraine? Rachel wondered. The ones who fell for Shane and those who comforted them when things fell through? If *she* was in love with Shane and he left her, she certainly wouldn't go crying to every other woman in town.

No, you would just quietly cry into your pillow every night. You'd deal with your broken heart by yourself. And right there, in Cynthia Corvellis's Handy House store, Rachel realized just how much danger she was sliding into. Already she was beginning to care about the man, barging into his business, looking forward to when he came in for lunch. She could almost feel the pain of losing Shane this very minute. Which was wrong. It couldn't be happening. She was not going to allow herself to care. No.

"Shane's not a bad man," Cynthia was telling her. "He's just not the marrying kind. The world needs all kinds, including men who don't settle down and who raise a little hell now and then. And...what can I say? He's ours. It's been years since I've really seen him. I'd like to say hello. Any chance you could talk him into coming into the store?"

Rachel opened her mouth to say no. "I'm not sure," she said instead. *Idiot!*

"He used to come here with his mother when she shopped for dry goods," Cynthia went on, a smile lighting her face. "I always had licorice whips on the counter and I always gave him one when they left the store. He was the cutest little boy and he loved those things. His eyes would positively light up. But...I guess he's too old for licorice whips now."

She sounded so wistful that Rachel found herself saying, "I'll bet he still loves them." And then she asked Cynthia to help her pick out some curtains. It was the least she could do, since she had made up that awful lie and since her attempts to bring Shane to Moraine had failed.

When she was through, Cynthia turned to her and said, "I'm sorry I implied that something was going on between you and Shane. That was wrong of me. I just...Shane was always in trouble, but I don't know...I just liked him. And he made things exciting, you know?"

"I know," Rachel agreed. There was an energy about Shane that turned a beige world flame-red. Oh, no, there were those dangerous thoughts again. "When I get back to the ranch," she said, "I'm going to tell Shane that Cynthia Corvellis helped me pick out his curtains. They really are lovely, Cynthia. Just what the room needs."

The older woman positively glowed at the compliment. "You enjoy them, sweetie," Cynthia said. But of course that wasn't going to happen. At least not for more than a few days. Then the curtains would be someone else's to enjoy.

Rachel said goodbye and exited the store, heading toward the car. Across the street she noticed two men watching her, one elderly and the other one not so elderly. There was no malevolence in their perusal of her, and she had a hunch they knew who she was.

Her first instinct was to ignore them and just hurry to her car. Nice as Cynthia had eventually turned out to be, Rachel didn't need any more people asking her if she was Shane's newest conquest. How many women had the man had when he was living here?

She turned to go. But then it occurred to her that maybe all of this whispering and gossiping was part of the reason Shane didn't want to come to town. And years of girls' school training kicked in. If there was going to be talk, she preferred to have the chance to be a part of the dialogue instead of the powerless recipient.

Crossing the street, she held out her hand. "Excuse me, I'm Rachel Everly. I'm working for Shane Merritt at Oak Valley Ranch."

"We know. We weren't trying to be rude by staring. We were just wondering how to approach you without seeming too forward," one of the men said, looking a bit sheepish. "I'm Len Hoskins. I own the drugstore. And this is Jarrod Ollis."

Rachel said hello to both of them. "What…is there something I can do for you?"

"We just wanted to ask how Shane is doing." Len took the lead again. "I hear he stopped in town one day when we'd already rolled up most of the streets, that he bought some supplies and hasn't been seen here since. I missed seeing him that time and I wonder, if he plans to make another trip to town, could you ask him to let us know? Or could you let us know? It's been ten years since he left Moraine."

"I'd hate to miss having the chance to trade stories with him," Jarrod agreed. "I mean, he *was* in town for his brother Eric's funeral a year ago, but the arrangements were made in advance and he barely made an appearance. Not that I blame him. Some people need to be private in their grief. Still, Shane and Eric made this town rock, and it's been pretty boring without them."

"They were something," Len said with a laugh. "Eric was captain of the football team and Shane was always tinkering with machines and breaking hearts. But then, you know all that."

No, she knew almost nothing. Still, Rachel made a small sound of assent.

"And fighting," Jarrod said with a smile, grabbing his jaw in a gesture that indicated Shane must have punched him there once. "Shane had a mean right hook, and he wasn't averse to getting down in the dirt to wrestle you if it came to that." Obviously it had come to that more than once. "Wouldn't mind sharing old stories with him."

"Why don't you?" Rachel asked, and immediately wondered if she should have said that. Darn her impulsive mouth. But it was said. She wasn't backing down now. "Why don't you talk to him?"

"We just told you, Rachel. He hasn't come to town."

"But you could go see him. You could drop by the ranch."

Wasn't that what people did in small towns? They dropped by when they wanted to say hello? Ruby seemed to imply that people were always welcome at her place even if they weren't staying or paying.

Jarrod rubbed his jaw again, looking vaguely worried. "I don't know about coming to the ranch. Might make him mad."

"If it does, I'll protect you from him," Rachel said, drawing a big laugh from Len.

"I think I like you, Rachel," he said. "But I'm not so sure about stopping by the ranch, either. If Shane wanted to see us, he'd come here. That's just the truth. If he's staying on the ranch, then he doesn't want to have anything to do with his neighbors. But tell him hey from Len."

"And from Jarrod," Jarrod said. "Tell him if he comes to town there'll be payback."

Rachel blinked.

"I'm lyin', of course," Jarrod said with a wink.

"Of course," she agreed. But she had a feeling that Jarrod rather enjoyed fighting.

She also had a feeling that she had dodged a bullet. Maybe. Clearly she had been wrong about ranch and small town etiquette. At least in this small town and in terms of this ranch.

Len and Jarrod were probably right that it was a bad idea. Shane didn't want to come to town. And the people *were* the town. No matter her feelings about leaving places and people on good terms, those were her beliefs, not his.

"Good thing no one's coming," she muttered on her way back. "Saved from my own impulsiveness by the good people of Moraine." She smiled. It occurred to her that she liked Shane's hometown better than he did.

It might not be a good idea to tell him that she'd messed up again and invited people to the ranch.

But, good idea or not, she would have to do it.

CHAPTER SEVEN

THE next day Shane came back to the house at lunch-time to find that Rachel had transformed his dining room into something...

"Livable," he said as he stared down at the table dressed in his mother's cream-colored tablecloth and topped with an old bottle green vase he hadn't seen in years. The vase was full of golden blossoms and there were cream and merlot candles scattered about.

"Livable?" she asked. "Is that good or bad? Is it praise? Maybe?"

"Sorry. Yes, it's praise," he said with a trace of a smile. "And don't pretend you don't know what I mean by livable. This place has only been inhabited by men since I was eight years old. Lately it's mostly been the home of mice. It had gone beyond functional to funky. And I don't mean that in a good way. So, yes, the fact that someone might actually eat or entertain in here by choice rather than necessity is a good thing."

She held out her hand. "Note the curtains."

They were nice—plain cream-colored curtains with bottle-green scalloped edging and tiebacks—but nothing to write ballads about.

"Cynthia Corvellis helped me pick them out," she said.

The name opened up a wound in his soul. Cynthia

had been Eric's piano teacher. She had adored Shane's brother. No question why. Eric had been the most lovable person on earth. According to everyone. According to me, Shane thought. *Don't think about it,* he thought.

"Cynthia always had good taste," he said.

"She's a nice woman," Rachel agreed. "She told me that you used to love licorice whips and she kept a container of them on the counter for you."

A tiny smile flickered over his lips, then died. "I know what you're doing, Rachel. Cynthia is a very nice woman. I'm happy that she helped you find what you needed. But I'm still not going to town."

"I know. What if town came to you, though?"

He froze. "Rachel, what do you mean?"

There was a pause. A long pause. "I might have done something you won't like."

He stared at her. He could tell that she was waiting for the whip to come down on her back. "What is it that you might have done?"

"I—I'm not sure. Maybe nothing." She told him about her conversations yesterday.

He studied the ceiling, fought for composure. The thought of trading stories with people who had known him when...

"Rachel, why would you do that after I'd specifically stated that I didn't want to go to town to meet my neighbors?"

She bit her lip and glanced to the side. "You didn't exactly say that you didn't want to meet them. You just said you didn't want to go to town."

Before he could say anything she rushed on. "No, that's not right or fair. I knew you weren't just avoiding the location. It's just that...friendship is such a valuable thing. I-it's not good to waste it, even if it lasts for only a very short time."

"More words of wisdom?" He blew out a breath.

"Yes," she said quietly. "I—I'm really sorry. I had no right to try to foist my ideas on you. And while I don't think that any of those people will actually show up—they seemed reluctant to invade your privacy— just in case, I'll get in touch with each one of them and explain that I was wrong to issue the invitation."

It was an eloquent little speech, a perfectly pretty speech. And Shane had no doubt that Rachel would follow through. She was naive and almost innocent in some ways, but tough when toughness was required. Tougher than he was, he thought. And what was the source of all that moral toughness? Of all her pretty and, yes, naive, little rules? He didn't know, but he knew that there was a sadness in her. He remembered that she had chosen to move to a state where she apparently knew no one.

"No. Leave it. Don't make the calls," he said. Because somehow he didn't like the idea of making Rachel humble herself to retract her invitation. "But Rachel?"

She waited.

"I'm sure the rules you live by are very nice and all, but don't try to turn me into something I'm not. Don't expect me to live by *your* rules."

"I won't," she said, her voice coming out soft and strained. "I promise."

That word. That word. The one word that meant so many awful things to him.

"Don't." He practically bit off the word. "Please, don't promise me anything."

He might as well have slapped her, he thought later.

Her eyes went puppy dog wounded, but to her credit she pulled herself together almost instantaneously.

"It was only an expression," she said. "I said it out of habit. It meant nothing."

But he knew that she was lying. Those little rules she used…he had no idea where they had come from, or when she had picked up the habit, but he knew that they meant something important to her. And he knew he'd been a total jerk.

His words had stolen Rachel's smile, her sunshine. And when it disappeared… When had he started looking forward to her smile? How long had he been waking up and anticipating her arrival at the house just because he coveted that smile?

He didn't know. He couldn't allow himself to think about that. Because in the end it couldn't matter. He and Rachel would be parting ways soon.

But he knew one thing. He needed to fix things and bring back Rachel's smile. If he could. He planned to concentrate on that this afternoon.

But then Rachel went missing.

Rachel needed advice, and she didn't want to go to Ruby. Ruby had known Shane for too long. She was a little biased. Plus there was the fact that she was a bit of a romantic. She would read something into Rachel's questions that wasn't there.

The perfect person would be someone who didn't know Shane very well. That was how Rachel ended up on Marcia's doorstep and how she ended up spilling her guts about what she had done.

"I just had to confess my sins to someone, and any woman who can decipher the ins and outs of Shane's antique appliances ranks as a practical sort of person who might give me practical advice," she said.

Marcia laughed at that. "Hank would probably disagree about the practical part. He thinks I'm a dreamer. But I see what you mean. It's always easier to be objective about other people's relationships than about your own."

Rachel froze in the act of lifting the cup of tea Marcia had just given her. "Shane and I don't have a relationship."

"Hmm, not sure I buy into that. That day at his house, the wattage on your smile turned up twice as high when he walked in. And I saw you looking at his biceps."

"I didn't."

Marcia drummed her fingers on the table. "I thought you wanted truth, objectivity."

"Okay. I do feel a little breathless when he's around. But it's probably just due to all the exercise I'm getting lately. And, anyway, I don't like it."

"Don't have to."

"This isn't solving my problem. I was hoping you could tell me what to do."

"About your infatuation with Shane?"

"About the possibility that I may have opened the door to unwanted visitors," she said, explaining what had happened. But when Marcia opened her mouth to speak, Rachel shook her head. "No, don't say anything. I was wrong. I thought I wanted advice, but then I've never been good at taking advice. I think what I really wanted was just someone to listen. I've been feeling a little tense lately."

"Because you're afraid you might fall in love with a man who can't offer you a future?"

"Not really."

Yes, Rachel thought. She'd had her heart scraped raw by people and she'd spent the past few years trying to learn to be smarter, less susceptible. Shane threatened that plan; he made her feel weak and wanton and afraid of what getting too close to him could do to her. But she was also afraid of more.

"I'm afraid of failing him. Somehow."

"Cooking? Cleaning?"

Rachel smiled a little. "Well, I fail on those counts every day, but that's not it. He seems like such a hard man, especially the way he's so set on dismantling and selling his childhood home, but he's not. And me with my blundering, acting without thinking ways… Just look at how I invited the world into his life when he's been trying to close it out. What damage I might have done. Maybe even now someone is driving toward Oak Valley and something terrible will happen. What kind of a woman would do something like that?"

"A loving one, Rachel. You had good intentions."

But good intentions didn't always count for much, she knew. "I'd better get back," she said. "I only meant to stay a few minutes."

"Okay, but can you at least stop and say hello to Ella and Henry? They've been dying to show you their goat."

Rachel's heart lifted immensely. "Lead me to the cherubs and Tunia. I wouldn't miss it. Mind if I snap some pictures of them?"

"They love smiling for the camera. And don't you dare forget to send me copies."

That was how Rachel ended up on her back, trying to get an upward shot of Ella and Henry, when another subject moved into her viewfinder.

"Hello, darlin'," Shane said. "Have I mentioned how much trouble you are?"

No, but lots of people had over the years. Rachel stared up at Shane and noted that his eyes seemed to be fiercer than usual. His frown was out in full force. Her immediate instinct was to scramble to her feet, because she was most definitely at a disadvantage lying on the ground. But that wasn't her way.

"Hello, Shane," she said. "I was just here collecting recipes in the hopes of saving your life." Which wasn't a lie. She had asked Marcia for some new "recipes for the hopeless" and she had them stashed in her camera bag.

"Were you, now?" He reached out and held a hand out. And even though Rachel knew how dangerous it was, touching Shane in any way, she placed her hand in his.

The kick was immediate. The tension traveled through her body quickly, clicking on every nerve ending, turning on that lust thing that she could never quite seem to control whenever Shane was around. But that was for her to know and no one to find out. "Thank you," she said as she regained her footing and Shane released her. Was that disappointment she was feeling when he let go of her?

"Sorry, munchkins," she told Ella and Henry. "Gotta get back to work."

Ella looked as if she was going to cry. She blinked hard and her lower lip trembled.

"Tunia?" Henry asked. "No Tunia?"

Shane dropped down beside them. "Was Rachel going to take a picture of Petunia?"

Henry nodded slowly. Shane picked him and Ella up and held one of them in each arm. "Well then, I apologize for interrupting. Rachel's yours for a few more minutes. Some things are way more important than lunch. Right?"

He got his answer when little Ella wrapped her arms around Shane's neck and hugged him while Henry patted him gently on the arm.

For no reason Rachel could think of, her chest suddenly felt tight. She tried to say "thank you" and had to clear her throat.

"Work your magic, Rachel," Shane said quietly. "I'll be waiting at the house when you get done."

Within minutes Rachel was struggling to capture the essence of the little lively goat and get Ella and Henry in the picture at the same time as all three of them jumped around with excitement.

"Did you get what you wanted?" Shane asked when she finally walked in the door.

"Yes," she said, thinking of the photos and the recipes and the companionship with Marcia. And, *no,* she thought, staring up into Shane's eyes and thinking of how messed up her heart was becoming and how there were no easy answers on how to protect herself or how to fix what she had messed up with him.

"Good," he said as he crossed the room. "I'm glad. But…please don't leave without at least telling someone where you've gone, Rachel. This is a ranch. There's water and rock, barbed wire and rough terrain. And heavy machinery that can hurt you. I didn't know where you were. I didn't know where to look."

His always deep voice was deeper, thicker. She looked up at him and her heart lurched at that dark, smoky and anguished expression. "I'm sorry," she said. "I didn't think."

"I know," he said. "But Rachel?"

She looked up.

"Next time…think. Tell someone. Tell me. Don't make me worry about you again. I've lost people on this ranch before." And then he placed one hand on the door frame she was standing next to. He kissed her. Hard. Fast. Done. The kiss was over almost as soon as it had begun.

"I'm not apologizing for that. I had to touch you."

Which made her heart hurt. He had lost people and she had gone missing on a ranch the size of Texas. The kiss had been a reassurance kiss. Nothing more.

"I won't wander off without notifying you again."

He nodded, and turned as if he was going to leave to go back to work. Instead, he stopped mid-stride and looked at her. "I'm glad that Marcia is close. You get lonely out here, don't you? That's what my mother used to say, that the ranch was a lonely place."

Rachel shook her head. "No, actually, I don't. That is, I love that Marcia is nearby, too, but…I like the ranch. I haven't felt lonely once." And she knew what loneliness was. She was on intimate terms with it.

"Still, you haven't seen much of the fun side of ranching. Come on." He took her by the hand and led her outside. It didn't take a cartographer to realize that he was leading her toward the corral. "Let's go see the horses. Lizzie misses you."

Rachel laughed at that. "I've gone to see the horses more than once since I've been here. I didn't notice that any of them had any special interest in me."

"That's because you haven't gotten close enough to talk to them."

"That's because they're big."

"But you can charm her. You have carrots."

"I do?"

Shane laughed. "Yes." He produced a carrot and showed her how to hold it on the flat of her palm so that her fingers couldn't get nipped by Lizzie's teeth. The horse lapped the carrot up and then snuffled around for more.

"Oh, she's hungry. Do you have another one?" Rachel asked.

"Yes, and she's not hungry. She knows you're a sucker. And you like to feed people."

"Lizzie, I promise you that these carrots are much healthier than my cooking and not nearly so lethal." The horse's gentle whinny seemed to say that she understood. Within no time Rachel and Lizzie seemed to be talking back and forth as Rachel rubbed Lizzie's coat. "I haven't really been out here much. I've been so busy."

"I know. I should have taken the time to make sure you had fun and not all work."

She shrugged. "I don't think bosses have to do that. Besides, there's that deadline."

"Even so, you've never been on a ranch, and you might not get near one again. I—Rachel, I won't push you, but...are you really afraid of Lizzie? I mean of riding Lizzie? Because I think you'd love it."

"I think I'd *want* to love it, but...I'm really, really terrified of heights. One of my stepmothers made me climb up on the roof when I was twelve because I'd thrown a Frisbee up there. I slipped and nearly fell off."

A low curse escaped Shane's lips. "That's criminal."

She shrugged, trying not to think about that day, an echo of her fear resounding in her memory even today. "I guess it wasn't a totally high roof. I practically dared her to make me do it. But still...I can't forget that swooping, out-of-control sensation as I gathered speed sliding toward the edge or the feeling that I might not be able to stop, trying to clutch at shingles and not being able to. Only my shoe jamming against the gutter saved me."

Shane's brows drew together. His hands were curled into fists. "Were you afraid of heights before?" The words shot from his mouth. Cold. Hard. Angry.

"No. I loved climbing."

He took deep, visible breaths, glancing down at the ground. Then he pinned her with his gaze. "I wouldn't presume to say I could help you forget that day. But... maybe I can help you take a baby step. I can hold Lizzie while you're up there. Rachel, horses and I...we go way back. They tell me their secrets. Lizzie likes you. She told me so."

He said the last in a whisper, conspiratorially, and Rachel knew he was trying to make her laugh, to distract her from her fears.

She looked up at the pretty horse with the gentle eyes. As if Lizzie understood, she gave a soft whicker.

"I don't know," Rachel said. "She looks really huge."

"Shh, you'll hurt her feelings. Lizzie worries that her rear end looks fat in a saddle."

Rachel couldn't hold back her smile then. "You have a lovely...um...rear end, Lizzie, but you're a bit taller than I am." Which wasn't saying much. Most people were a bit taller than she was.

Again as if she understood, Lizzie tossed her head. She gave Rachel another one of those sad looks. If she didn't know better, Rachel would have thought that Shane was coaching the pretty creature.

"Will you promise not to let me fall?" she asked Shane.

"No."

She blinked wide, startled.

"Sometimes you fall when you're on a horse," he said. "And I hate it when people promise what they can't deliver. Let's just say that I'll do my best to make sure you don't end up facedown in the dirt. And, if you do, I'll pick you up and dust the grass off of you."

"Ah, Ruby was right that first day. You're a real sweet-talker, Shane," she said.

He smiled. "You're stalling. And you know you want to try. I'm betting that a belief that trying new things is healthy is one of those handy little sayings you fling about."

"It's not," she said. "But it probably should be. Okay, I'm willing to try…once. Show me how to do this," she told him.

Within a very short time Shane had wandered off and located a pair of boots that were a size too big, but which served the purpose. He had her up on Lizzie's back. "Lizzie's no youngster, so she'll be slow. She won't run off with you."

In fact Lizzie was standing quietly, seemingly unperturbed to have Rachel on her back. Rachel felt the big animal's muscles shift beneath her and her breath caught in her throat. She reached out to touch Lizzie's back. "I'm counting on you, Lizzie," she whispered. "No bad surprises." She'd certainly had enough of those in her life.

"Let's try a leisurely walk down to the corral and back," Shane said, and he showed her what to do. To Rachel's surprise, Lizzie did just as she was asked.

"Are you giving her some secret commands?" she asked Shane.

He laughed. "She's just responding to *your* commands. You're letting her know what you want and she knows the drill."

Rachel knew that there wasn't anything magical about riding a horse. People had been doing it for years. But there was something so heady about asking her horse partner to take her somewhere and having Lizzie do exactly as she asked. She held the power, she had control in ways she'd rarely ever been in control during her life. Riding this slowly was simple stuff, feeling powerful because of it was silly, and yet...

"I like this," she said. "I can feel her moving and it's as if we're a team."

"You *are* a team."

But they were a slow team, probably a very slow team. Rachel was pretty sure that an experienced person like Shane wouldn't have been moving at anything near this crawl if not for her. "I should be working," she said suddenly. "I'm keeping you from what you need to do."

"Not true. The horses are an integral part of the ranch and they need to be exercised. You're helping."

"If this is as much exercise as Lizzie gets, she's going to start putting on some pounds real soon. Maybe we should go faster." She couldn't help the hopeful sound in her voice.

Shane laughed. "Not now. Those boots don't even fit you. You might fall if we speed things up." But they did speed up...just a bit. And she didn't fall.

She fell in love with Lizzie and with horseback riding and with Oak Valley. Beyond that, Rachel refused to think, but when Shane lifted her from the saddle and slid her down to the ground, her body touching his, it was all she could do to keep from wrapping her arms around his neck and begging him to kiss her. Thank goodness there wasn't too much time left with Shane or there was no question that she was going to be in serious, heart-shattering trouble.

CHAPTER EIGHT

WHEN Rachel arrived at Oak Valley the next day, Shane noticed two things. She was wearing his favorite smile and...

"I like the boots," Shane said. "Did you pick those out all by yourself?"

To his delight, she blushed, just as he'd known she would. Rachel always looked pretty, but when she blushed she was darn near irresistible. Which was a good sign that he shouldn't be trying to make her blush, but...those boots...

"As a matter of fact, I did pick them out," she said, lifting her chin in a defiant gesture. "I liked the blue flowers curling around the instep. They look pretty against the golden leather, and, yes, I *was* told that they were impractical and that they would get dirty, that they were really more for rodeos and things like that, but I bought them anyway."

He smiled. "Impulsive. Stubborn."

She sighed. "Yes, but I bought them because...it's just that I'll probably never have another pair of cowboy boots. If I'm only going to have one...well, you know."

"You don't seem like the type of woman who allows

anyone to dictate her style. You could wear boots for the rest of your life."

"I know. But it would be different then. I would just be posturing. These boots are going to be real. I'm going to actually use them. If Lizzie lets me back in the saddle."

Shane shook his head, confused. "Why wouldn't she?"

Rachel laughed then, that spontaneous, pretty, bell-like sound that turned his body hot. "I think I might have bored her to death yesterday. Next time you show me how to keep her entertained."

"Entertained?" Shane couldn't hold back his grin. "Rachel, I don't think I've ever met anyone who worried about whether the ranch animals were having fun. Lizzie is a working horse."

"Who hasn't been working for a while."

"Can't argue that."

"Do you think she'll mind getting moved around again when the ranch sells? I mean, she lived here with you, then she got moved to the other stable. Now she's here again. But for how long? Someone might buy her and take her elsewhere. Do you think that horses feel stressed about moving around the way people do?"

Shane hesitated. She had injected the subject of the ranch selling, the only reason they were here and something that was quickly coming up on the calendar. And she was right, too. "Yes, I think they do feel stress. Are you trying to guilt me into making sure that Lizzie stays here, Rachel?" Not that he blamed her. The truth was that he *had* felt guilty about moving the horses away from their home.

Rachel looked up, her eyes wide. "I don't know.

I was just wondering. I—seriously, I'm sorry about that."

"Don't be. You're right. I'll do what I can to make sure this experience is as stress free as possible for them. Now, I have a few things I want to discuss with you this morning. Have a seat."

She sat, and he noticed the sunlight glinting off her hair. She was as lovely as one of her photos, he thought. He wished he could capture this image and hold it, but...

"Let's discuss the schedule, first of all," he said, and he told her what he had done and what he had left to do. "The house is looking very inviting. Warm," he added. "You've made a big difference here."

"Thank you. I wanted it to feel like a home," she said softly.

The very words made his heart hurt. This house had never been a home, and he knew from things she'd said in the past how much she wanted one. Louise, his Realtor friend, had called him last night.

"Louise told me that she thinks she's found you an apartment and that you concur."

"Louise is a genius."

"She is. So, tell me, what are your plans when you move to Maine?" The days were flying past, and it had occurred to him—several times—that Rachel was rootless. She had her dream of a home, but she'd left her job with Dennis. "Do you have another job as a photographer lined up?"

Those brown eyes flickered. "Shane, I think I may have mentioned that I'm not really a pro. You've seen my work. It's adequate, but not more."

It *was* more.

"In fact," she said, "I've been meaning to ask—"

Now she looked nervous, her tongue sliding over her lip in a way that was driving him crazy. He took a deep breath. "Ask."

"Those shots I took of the ranch…I know they're not great and I was wondering if you wanted me to redo any of them. I don't want to fail you."

That was it. Shane sat down and took her hands in his. "Rachel, I don't need art to sell this ranch. The shots of the ranch are good. If I was going to buy a ranch, your photos would sell me on this one." He glanced at one she had hung on the wall, the one with the field of flowers. "Who wouldn't want to stare at that every day?" he asked. "But…" He could feel her fingers tense beneath his own. "Who made you so unsure of your talent? Was it that stepmother who nearly killed you?"

"That sounds *über*-dramatic, like Hansel and Gretel." She was trying to make a joke, to keep it light, and Shane wanted to give her what she wanted, but ever since yesterday he'd known that bad things had happened to her. Her stepmother had sent her onto a roof and he didn't care how "not very high" it had been. It had certainly been high enough to have made her fearful.

"Rachel, you're a trouper. You're a tough one. But…I need to know that you'll be safe and settled when we part. I need to know how you ended up on a roof. And that something like that won't happen to you again. Because I won't be there to try and save you, and that's going to make me insane."

"Don't," she said, pulling her hand away. "Don't pity me or feel responsible for me. I don't like even mentioning this stuff. I never tell anyone. But if it will keep you from worrying, I'll tell you this much.

I had...*have* self-absorbed parents who didn't want a child. So, as soon as I was old enough, they sent me to boarding schools. Lots of them. They moved me around on whims. And they married and divorced over and over, always trying to one up each other in the spouse department. I was called home when I might serve a useful purpose, such as sealing a deal with a potential new husband or wife. So, *yes,* there have been some bad moments and one or two bad stepparents. And, yes, my life has been rootless and unpredictable, and I've never stayed in one place long enough to have lasting friendships. But I don't need or want pity or concern. I learned how to make friends fast and how to jump in and figure out how to make each place my own quickly. Above all, I know how to take care of myself."

"I think that's clear. I'm amazed at how much you've accomplished here."

"One gets to be self-sufficient."

"I don't think many people would have such an optimistic outlook as you do. You're an amazing woman, Rachel."

She looked to the side. "What?" he asked, seeing that she was upset.

"I think you might have really meant that," she said.

Now he was angry. "Hell, yes, I did. You can't tell me that no one's ever said something similar to you."

"Dennis did. He said my photos were almost as good as his."

Little angry fires started in Shane's soul. "Dennis is a snake. And he's wrong about your photos."

Her head whipped around. "You don't like them?"

He smiled, just a little. "You know I do. What I meant was that I looked Dennis up online. Your photos put his to shame. Especially the ones with Ella and Henry. Hank showed me what you sent to Marcia last night and…you're amazing with children. You must have taken a hundred shots to catch the perfect expression. They were stunning, far beyond anything Dennis has ever produced. I suspect he knew that you are better than he is."

She gave a tiny nod, but she didn't look happy despite his compliment.

"So what do you plan to do in Maine?" he asked, getting back to what was worrying him even more now that he knew about her parents.

"I'll land on my feet. I always make sure that I do."

"That's not good enough."

"It's all I've got."

"Then you're selling yourself short."

"I don't think so. I know what I can and can't do."

"I don't want to know what you can do. I want to know what you're really *going* to do. Whether you like it or not, I'm going to worry if you're not set up with a way to feed yourself."

She shrugged. "I'm sorry. I really am. I wish I could tell you, but I'd just be making stuff up. I won't know until I'm there, facing reality."

"So it's just do or die when you get there? That works for you?"

"Well, it keeps me in food. I'm not dead yet."

Shane frowned.

"I'm sorry. I shouldn't have said that. It was insensitive."

"Don't. You don't have to muzzle yourself for me. But, yeah, I hate that when you leave here you'll be standing on a ledge waiting to see which side of the drop-off the wind will blow you to. So…how about this? It's not unusual for writers or artists to have another career to keep them solvent. With your natural way with children you could be a teacher. Maybe an art teacher. You'd be a sure success at something like that, and I just thought…why don't you go to college and explore your options?"

She didn't look convinced. "I did begin college right after I got out of school. My mother stopped paying the bills, and without a loan or a grant I was left hanging. Then she insisted that she was desperately ill and I needed to come home and help her."

"*Was* she ill?"

"Sort of. She'd had a face-lift and then she'd fallen while she was ignoring the doctor's orders to slow down. So I went home." The way she said it led Shane to believe that it wasn't the first time something like that had happened.

"She doesn't have servants?"

"When Mother is between husbands she tends to fire her servants. Me, she can't fire. It's why I'm such a hot commodity with the parents when they're between spouses and need someone to listen to them. Anyway, from there we went overseas for a year, and by the time we returned and Mother had met a man, I was two years behind. I got a job at a camera shop and never went back to college. Now it feels too late."

"You're twenty-five. I've met people who went back in their fifties. People have gone to college in their seventies."

"It takes money."

"You'll get a loan."

"I have to work so that I can eat."

"So, take classes when you can. In fact…start now."

Rachel frowned, confused.

"You can get some of your gen eds via web-based classes. Rachel, why not try? You can still keep working at your craft—it would be a total shame for the world to lose your art—but security can also be a very good thing."

"Says the man who changes addresses every six weeks."

"True. But I *am* always gainfully employed when I move."

"Touché. I'm seldom gainfully employed, even though I'd like to be."

"The world needs more people like you at the helm, Rachel. More spit in the eye people, more enthusiastic people. Some lucky employer is going to be fortunate to get you."

"I don't know. I've gone to so many schools. I—"

"Is that it? Because you're not coming in as a freshman you'll feel like the new girl again?"

"I—yes."

"That's the beauty of college. People transfer all the time. Go to a big school. Lots of other people are guaranteed to be new, too. You won't be the only one. Just…think about it."

She didn't answer.

"Rachel?"

"I'm thinking about it," she said. "Seriously. I'm thinking about it."

Apparently that was as good an answer as he was going to get, Shane realized. He wanted to be happy with that answer. For her sake he would have to accept it.

But happy?

No. He couldn't be happy knowing that Rachel could simply disappear off the face of the earth and there wasn't a thing he could do about it. That had happened to him before.

This situation with Rachel might not be life or death, but having her vanish and be swallowed up where he might never even be able to locate her still promised to be incredibly painful.

Rachel was trying not to think about the fact that she had spilled her guts to Shane. She'd never done that before and now she felt naked. Uncertain. So she was throwing herself into work, trying to avoid the big questions about his suggestion, but mostly…him.

The calendar days were dropping off. Goodbye was right around the corner and she didn't want to think about it. So today she'd tackle one of her last cleaning tasks. She had almost worked her way to the back of the massive hallway closet, which housed decades of coats, mittens and hats. Boxes of greasy tools shared shelf space with old jelly jars with no lids. Torn and yellowed journals on ranching contained articles on such subjects as the pros and cons of different types of fencing.

"Pitch it all," Shane had said whenever she'd asked him about anything she found in the various storage spaces in the house.

And she was in the process of doing just that when she came upon a large black lacquered box with an ivory scrimshaw cameo of a woman set into the lid. When she opened it up it smelled faintly of tea, as if that was what had once been housed there. But there was no tea in the box, just lots and lots of packets of seeds. The box was so full that when Rachel opened it some of them fell out. Phlox and pinks, zinnias and sunflowers, columbine and daisies, delphiniums and marigolds. The once brightly colored packets were slightly faded now, and a few of them were opened. She took them out and spread them out on the table. At the bottom of the box were charts outlining where each plant would find a home.

Pitch it all, she heard Shane saying. But…

Gathering up her find, she went in search of Shane and found him repairing an overhead light in the tool-shed. He was standing on a ladder, his arms over his head, the muscles in his back beneath his white shirt tensing with his movements.

For a moment she just watched him…until she realized that she was looking like some ridiculous plain-Jane schoolgirl salivating over a boy who would inevitably never notice that she was even in the room.

She cleared her throat, loudly.

And Shane hit his head on the light fixture. A string of low curses dropped from his mouth and he turned around.

Heat traveled up from her toes, making all of her feel…hot. Very hot. She knew she was blushing. Horrid habit. Why couldn't she just control her body's reactions to the man?

"I'm so sorry," she said. "I startled you."

"Don't apologize. You were just trying to let me know you were there. I'm the one who swore the air blue. I'm the one who's sorry."

Then he smiled, and her inner schoolgirl emerged again. She held out the box mutely.

His smile disappeared. He came down from the ladder slowly.

"Where did you find this?" he asked.

"Buried in the hallway closet. It must have been in there a very long time. The colors on the packages are faded. I know you told me to throw everything in there away, but this seemed...special. The box is very pretty, unique, probably expensive. And the seeds..." The seeds interested her more than the box. "There are so many of them, and there are these wonderful planting charts with comments like 'Phlox reminds me of home,' or quotations by Wordsworth like 'Daisies: The Poet's Darling' scribbled in the margins of the charts."

She stared up at him, waiting for him to tell her about this treasure, because it was obvious that he knew what it was. But the look in his eyes...was it pain? Was it remembrance? "Were these yours?" she asked. "Or...?"

"My mother's. I remember her planting a garden every year. She could never have enough and always tried to cram too many into the space she had plotted out. If a frost came she would run out in the night and try to cover everything up. I remember my stepfather, Frank, chiding her for that. 'Flowers aren't that important,' he told her."

"But they are," Rachel said. "Even if you're sad, a flower can cheer you up. Not that I know anything of gardens. I never had one. My mother...well, you know about my mother. She would be horrified at the thought of kneeling down in the dirt. And I was never in one place long enough to plant one of my own. There would have been no place for a garden, anyway."

"Rachel..."

"No. That was bad of me. That sounded self-pitying and I'm not. I hate that kind of thing. It makes me feel small and icky. Besides, flowers are everywhere. I've had my share."

"From men?" Shane was wearing that smoky look again, the one that made it hard to breathe...or talk.

She gave him a haughty look. "I—I don't need a man to give me flowers," she managed to say. "They were mostly from me to me. Those count."

"They do. They count a lot."

She glanced down at the box. "This was your mother's. Not like the other stuff in the closet. What should I do with it?" She held it out to him. "You should keep it. Seriously. Just this one thing."

He placed his hands over her own, shook his head and slowly restored the box to her arms. "No, I want you to keep it. Please."

"But it's special. It's your mother's."

"It *is* special. And my mother would have liked it to be used by a gardener. When you get to Maine and find a bit of land, plant your own garden. The seeds won't grow. They're too old. But you'll fill the box with your own. That's a much more fitting end to it than sitting on a shelf in my apartment or hotel room. And someday you'll have flowers."

But the very next day she had flowers. Several vases of them arrived. When she approached Shane to thank him, he looked sheepish. "Have to have flowers for an open house," he said.

"You're a softie, Shane Merritt," she said. "You know these won't last that long. You just did this because I told you I hadn't had any flowers from a man."

"I did it because I can't believe what a low class of men you must have been hanging around with if none of them sent you flowers."

She smiled. "Well, I've obviously met a higher class of man now."

He scowled. "No. You haven't. This was bribery, pure and simple. Now, let's get back to work."

She did, but several times that day she stopped to

bury her nose in the flowers. She tried to remind herself that these weren't special. Shane had surely sent
flowers to many women. And would again long after
all she had left of him were memories.

Her heart hurt. She really needed to think about the
future.

Soon.

Rachel wandered through the next few days in a fog
of gratitude and pain and regret. She had finally taken
Shane's suggestions to heart and had enrolled in an
online class. It was a small start, but maybe it would
be something to look forward to when she was tempted
to look back to her days on the ranch. That was the
gratitude part.

For the rest…

"He's not coming, is he?" Ruby asked one day.
"Let's face it. He's going to leave here and never come
back and we'll never see him again."

"Ruby…" Rachel said, her heart breaking for the
woman.

"I know he has a good life and a good business,
but…I don't know. You watch a child grow up and
become a man, you have a part in his life, and… I
don't have any children of my own. I never married.
So the children in town are the closest I'll ever get to
having my own. I know I'm not the only one, either. It
was awful when Eric died. He was so young. He'd been
engaged, but he'd barely become an adult. He didn't
leave us by choice. Shane's refusal to interact with us…
it feels a lot like rejection," Ruby said.

Rachel's throat was closing up. She'd been dealing
with the reality of leaving Shane for days, maybe ever
since she'd come here. And, no matter how much she

wanted to deny it, she'd developed feelings for him. Feelings she was doing her best to shut out. She had no choice. She wasn't free to care. A man like Shane, who had told her from the first that he liked his life unfettered...falling for a man like that would be like ripping your own heart out voluntarily.

But Ruby...wonderful, warmhearted, fun and funny Ruby, who seldom was serious...to see her this way...

And Shane...whatever was keeping him from people like Ruby had to be something that hurt him badly. She knew he wasn't a man who would harm someone uncaringly.

Swiping her hand across her eyes hastily lest Ruby see the tears that threatened to fall, Rachel made a resolution. One way or another she was going to confront Shane about the way he was ignoring his neighbors and ignoring his own history. And punishing himself, she supposed, for youthful indiscretion.

And if he fired her...

She took a deep breath. *Well, I'm going anyway,* she reasoned. But she didn't want to think about that. Like everyone else, she wanted every last drop of time she could get with Shane.

Still, she would take the risk. He wasn't going to be happy about her intrusion into his life again.

Too bad.

Rachel sat at the kitchen table waiting for Shane to come in for dinner. Her stomach felt as if a million miniature gymnasts were staging a show, doing cartwheels and handstands and stealing all of her air. She had waited until this late hour so that there would be time, but she didn't relish making Shane angry; the fact that he was late only added to her nerves. Why was he late? Shane was not a man who showed up late with no explanation. She remembered his lecture about the dangers of ranching.

The phone rang loudly, startling her. "Rachel?" he yelled as she picked it up.

"Shane, what's wrong?" His voice was strained, and she could hear air whishing past, so he was moving fast as he talked. He was incredibly late for dinner. Fear lurched through her.

"I'm not coming in." He sounded as if he was running. "Rambler's hurt. I—does blood make you faint?"

"It never has before."

"Good. The vet's on another call, Tom's on the outskirts of the property, Hank's getting over a cold and I'd rather not risk any more infection here. Meet me at the barn."

She didn't hesitate. She just ran, her legs pumping fast as she entered the barn to find Shane already there examining the horse with gentle yet persistent movements. At the sound of her entrance, he rose.

"You need to wash up," Shane told her. He gestured to a sink and soap and began to scrub his hands. "I won't need you to do more than hand me things, but I don't want any extra germs."

Rachel did as he said. She glanced at Rambler, who was clearly in distress, and at Shane's tense expression. "Tell me what you need."

"Saline first. Some sterile gauze, bandages and disinfectant." He grabbed the saline and moved off toward the horse, clearly expecting her to follow. She scrambled to locate the other supplies and hurried over to where he was kneeling, next to the frightened and quivering animal.

"Shh, boy. How'd you do this, anyway? Were you

dreaming of some pretty little filly and not paying attention to where you were going? It's okay, Rambler. We all get hurt now and again." As he spoke, his words soft and low and soothing, he gently washed the wound with saline, pressing his body against the horse's, calming him. "But I'll make it right. You'll heal. You're going to be just fine, boy. I know it hurts, but we're going to do our best to make that better right away."

As he spoke, he gestured to Rachel, who handed him whatever he was pointing to. He kept up the low, gentle conversation as he worked. "Just a little bit longer, boy," he said, as he made the final wrap of the bandage. "I know this disinfectant doesn't smell pretty, like Lizzie, but it'll do the trick. Soon you'll be galloping off around the fields faster than ever. You'll play Romeo again. You'll be just fine."

He stood, straightening to his full height and patting the giant horse's side. As he did, Rambler tossed his head just a bit. "Oh, already feeling a bit better?" Shane asked. "Or are you just showing off for Rachel?"

Rambler whickered weakly, just as if he was answering, and Rachel finally realized that she was standing next to a creature much bigger and wilder than Lizzie. But…what could she do? The animal was hurt. That had been a nasty cut.

"Will he really be all right?" she asked.

"He'll be sore for a few more days, but he should be fine. The wound looked bad because of the blood, but it wasn't deep. Thank you,' he said. "I didn't want to ask for your help, but I wasn't sure what I was dealing with when I first got here."

"You're very good with horses, aren't you?" she asked. "You calmed him. He knew you'd take care of him. There was something rather beautiful about the whole experience. The man caring for his horse."

He shrugged. "Practice," he said. "This was nothing."

"Not to Rambler." And not to her, either. But as her words trailed off, Shane finished up in Ramber's stall, peeled off his bloody shirt and began to wash off. The muscles of his chest were slick as he reached for a towel.

Rachel closed her eyes. When she opened them again, he was staring at her with a fierce expression. He has clearly seen her looking at him.

"I should go back to the house," she said, her voice weak.

Shane nodded. And then he smiled that glorious dimpled smile. "I'll be right up. We can share a meal and celebrate your successful baptism as a veterinary assistant. Another notch on your résumé."

He looked happy. But Rachel knew that he wouldn't be happy for long. She still had to do what she had sworn she'd do today.

CHAPTER NINE

SHANE was just taking his last bite of Surprise Casserole, or, as Rachel called it, Super Surprise Casserole, when he looked up to find Rachel watching him with worried eyes.

She'd been quiet throughout the meal. He was pretty sure he knew what the problem was.

"Rachel, I apologize for asking you to help me with the horse. I know you're a city girl, that you're not very comfortable with large animals and that Rambler's much bigger than Lizzie. Believe me, if there had been anyone else around I wouldn't—"

She had placed her hand on his wrist, and now those big brown eyes were looking at him as if she was going to tell him something very bad.

He'd seen that look in someone's eyes twice before in his life. "Something's wrong."

"It's Ruby."

His heart dropped like a rock in water. "She's sick? She's hurt? No, you wouldn't have waited to tell me that—"

"Shane, no. It's nothing like that. It's just…she's depressed and hurt that you would come here and then leave without seeing her. And she's not alone. I know that whatever happened here, whatever made you hate this place so much is none of my business, but…I just can't leave this alone."

"Did she ask you to talk to me?"

"She didn't have to. She told me that she had no children and you and Eric had been like her children. And…it's not just that. I know part of why you hate this place has to be tied up with your brother and that room. I just… You've done so much for me. You've helped me so much and I… Shane, I'll be gone in four days. You'll be gone. And I know I'm just your house-keeper, I don't have a right to your personal business, but—"

He rose from the table, knocking his chair over in the process. Anger washed over him. At himself. At how Rachel was trying so hard to help him, to help Ruby and the others, and how he was mucking it all up. Again. As he had done before.

"You know you're not just a housekeeper. Damn it, Rachel. You just helped me bandage an animal that weighs ten times what you do. You've taken on tasks I know you had no interest in. You've befriended my neighbors."

"I just don't want to overstep—"

"You're not. It's not your fault you've been driven to this. Come on. It's time."

"Time for what?" Those big brown eyes looked un-certain.

"Time for several things. You're leaving in just a few days. So am I. But when you're gone I want you to take some memories. Some real ranch memories. And I want you to leave here knowing exactly what kind of man I am. Ruby plays me like some bad boy who's good at heart, but I'm not that guy."

"Who are you, then?"

"I'm a guy who made some serious mistakes and I can't ever forget them or forgive myself."

"Are we talking about Eric?" She looked toward the room.

Shane's heart hurt. His throat hurt. He knew the little-boy items that were in that room, pieces of his brother's past, baby pictures, so many things frozen in time. He just…couldn't do this here.

"Rachel, I need to be outside tonight, if you don't mind. Will you come with me? Will you…mind?"

To his consternation, she didn't hesitate. "I'll come."

He frowned. "You should hesitate. Not follow blindly. I need to know that you'll be safe when I'm gone, not just walking into danger without thinking."

"I was thinking. I was thinking that I trust you."

He scowled. "See, that's a mistake right there. You call Ruby and you tell her that I'm taking you out to Settler's Creek, to the camp zone. And that I'll have you back bright and early tomorrow morning. That's called insurance, Rachel. You always let someone know where you're going. When you'll return. Will you do that?"

"Only because Ruby will worry if I don't."

He wanted to swear, but he knew Rachel needed her independence. It was one of the things he loved about her.

That acknowledgment made him flinch. It wasn't her fault that he had done what he'd said he'd never do: fall in love. She would never know. He wasn't mixing another person up in his life, especially not Rachel, who was finally, finally, for once in her life, catching a break and on the road to realizing her dreams.

"Will you mind if we ride? I'll ask Tom to check in

on Rambler, but Cobalt needs exercise and Lizzie is always available for you."

"I'll get ready," she said, and soon they were on their way across the fields to the spot she'd once told him would be perfect for a cowboy fantasy.

But fantasies weren't on the menu tonight. Truth was. Rachel deserved truth. All of it. She'd been bleeding for his sin, trying to make things right with his neighbors, and he wasn't going to make her do that anymore.

When they got to the camp area he lifted her down from Lizzie and while he savored the chance to hold her in his arms, he didn't allow himself the kinds of thoughts he always had with Rachel. Instead, he spread a blanket and made a place for her to sit. Then he began to gather firewood.

"I can help," she said, starting to rise.

"No. Not tonight. Tonight you're my cowgirl guest. You stare at the mountains and watch as the stars begin to come out." He knelt by the cleared space and began to stack the wood.

"Shane?"

He looked up from his task. The last drops of sunlight were squeezing from the sky, and the fire-pink reflected back in Rachel's eyes. She looked more beautiful than ever, this tough-sweet woman. But she wasn't staring at the glorious sunset. She was looking at him. Was she trembling? Was he making her nervous?

"I'll keep the tale short," he said. "And then for the rest of the night you can just enjoy the beauty of the sky. That is, unless you want to go home after you've heard my story."

"In the dark?"

"I've got provisions and a lantern. I'd keep you safe."

"I know you would."

He breathed in deeply, wondering what he had done to deserve the appearance of Rachel in his life. But he already knew the answer to that. He didn't deserve her. He'd simply been lucky that day; he'd been blessed.

Now that was over. He'd had his turn. He reached for the last piece of wood, set fire to the kindling and waited for the flames to build. Then he took a place on the blanket, facing her. Not near enough to touch.

And he ripped off the bandage he had placed over his heart long ago. He began to speak.

Rachel realized right away that Shane had placed his back to the fire so that his face was in the shadows and hers was in full light. He'd made it clear that this was not a conversation that he relished. He was doing this because she'd asked. No, she'd needled, practically demanded. And as he began speaking, even though she couldn't see his expression, she could hear the change in his voice.

He was in pain. Real pain.

"My birth father was friends with my stepfather, and when my mother got pregnant and my father disappeared, Frank stepped in. He'd loved my mother from the first and eventually, when I was three, she married him even though she didn't love him. She did it for me, so that I would have security."

"Because she loved you."

"Yes. I don't think she would have agreed to the marriage otherwise. I was four when Eric was born, and eight when my mother died from an infected wound. One day she was there, the next day she was dying. By then, it was obvious that Frank didn't like me at all. I was a symbol of the man my mother really loved. And I was also the healthy brother. Eric was frail when he was young and he followed me around everywhere. Everywhere."

Shane's voice cracked a bit. He turned away slightly and waited until he had himself under control. "As she lay dying, feverish and weak and scared, my mother begged me to promise that I would watch over Eric. I think she had grown to loathe Frank, and she was afraid that a man who revered ranching and physical strength as much as he did would grow to hate his fragile son even more than he hated me. And by then she knew that I was the strong one. I was terrified and sobbing but I gave her my promise."

Rachel couldn't hold back her murmur of distress. "You were just a child."

He shook his head. "I was never a child. I had an attitude and a serious disregard for authority figures and rules. I learned to swear and spit, kick and bite, and ignore authority. But I took my responsibility to Eric seriously. And my little brother was my polar opposite. He was the friendliest, most lovable guy, like a big puppy or a very generous friend. He'd give you everything he owned if you'd let him, he'd lend a hand wherever it was needed and he surprised everyone by eventually shedding his fragility. He became an athlete, an outdoorsman, a true rancher, not an angry, spiteful math nerd who felt stuck on the ranch like I did."

"In other words he became the son Frank wanted."

"Yes."

"And you were the troublemaker, the one who wouldn't fit the mold."

"I was arrogant and angry at everyone, including my mother for dying, and especially at Frank for insisting he would turn me into a rancher or die trying. He hated the fact that I liked math and science more than raising cattle. I did anything I could to keep from doing the right thing...except where Eric was concerned."

Rachel could understand Shane regretting his wild childhood, but...the other...the way he still flagellated himself and shut himself off long after his tormentor was gone...

"Did your stepfather beat you?" She heard the horror in her voice.

"No. That wasn't Frank's way. That might have brought strangers to our door, and Frank didn't like strangers. No, Frank was a man of words, slurs, derision. But in public, in the rare times we appeared together, he never said a word. No one ever knew what went on here, and if they did...it wasn't illegal. A man can tell his sons whatever he wants to tell them.

"The only thing was...as I got older my arguments with Frank became more heated, and more frightening to Eric, who hated conflict of any kind. The day I brought him to his knees, begging me to please just go to my room and let Frank bellow, I decided that it was time to go. I tried to tell myself that it was for Eric's sake, but the truth was that I felt trapped. By my life, by Frank and..."

He stopped, looked up, clenching his fists.

"You felt trapped by your promise to take care of your brother?"

"Yes. I told myself he was old enough, but he was only sixteen, and I know my leaving hurt him. Tore him up."

Shane stopped again, trying to regain his composure. Rachel waited, silent.

"After that," he continued, "I only saw Eric away from here, I'd ask him to come to my hotel. Once or twice I flew him out to where I was. But I had stopped watching over him. And then Frank died, and Eric truly was alone, but I still didn't come home."

"How old was Eric then?"

"Twenty-two."

"A man."

"You wouldn't say that if you'd known Eric. He was a late bloomer, young for his age."

"But a talented rancher and outdoorsman."

Shane ignored that comment. "He met a girl, fell in love, got engaged. They were having a party. I was supposed to come, but I got snowbound and missed it. I sent flowers, and when the snow melted I just went back to work. The next day Eric went out to the field with the tractor to feed the cattle alone. He wouldn't have gone alone if he hadn't been upset with me. I'm sure of that. Eric was very safety conscious. And while he was pitching the hay to the cattle in a snow-covered field something went wrong. The tractor tipped and he was pinned beneath it. Crushed."

"You blame yourself?"

"Of course I'm to blame. I left him alone at sixteen, living with an uncommunicative and sullen father. I ignored his life as if only mine mattered. I might as well have been driving that tractor that took him to his death, because *I* had always been the reckless one, not him. He learned that maneuver, that wildness, from me. Because I cared too much about myself to care about anyone else."

"Is that why you avoid the people of Moraine? Because they witnessed all of what you consider your sins?"

"Not because they witnessed them. Because they were my victims. I wronged them over and over, cared nothing for their feelings and then I took their brightest sun, the best that Moraine had to offer. Eric was the boy who took in stray animals, he served as a make-shift vet when the real vet was unavailable, he shoveled people out of the snow. He was the go-to guy when anyone needed a strong shoulder, the peacemaker. And I hurt him so much that he…he died. Rachel, he *died*."

Rachel couldn't help herself then. She crawled across the blanket and wrapped her arms around Shane. She just held him while he wrestled with his demons. Silently struggling.

Eventually, when he seemed calmer, she looked up and kissed him on the chin. "The people of Moraine don't blame you, Shane, or if they ever did, they've forgiven you."

He looked down into her face. "I know. I've known that all along."

Oh, this was bad. This was difficult. "That's why you won't let them in? Because they've forgiven you but you haven't forgiven yourself? You don't want them to forgive you."

"I don't deserve their forgiveness."

Rachel didn't know what to say. She had spent a lot of time in her life learning how to deal with adversity and unhappy situations, loneliness, friends who could only be friends for the short term, but this was beyond her experience. And yet she couldn't let it go. This was Shane. This was…the man she cared for far too much, and it was impossible to leave things as they were.

"I know you loved your brother, Shane, but Eric was an adult. He made a choice."

Shane didn't answer.

"If he loved you—and I'm sure he did—he wouldn't want you to be this way."

Still no answer.

"Shane?"

"Rachel, do me a favor."

"What?"

"Don't— please don't try to save me. Just lie here with me beneath the stars. No touching. Nothing like that. Just be here with me."

"Anything," she said, her heart breaking.

He pulled her into his arms and lay down with her. "This isn't the romantic evening under the stars you once mentioned."

No, it wasn't, but she was right where she wanted to be. Not that she could tell him that. Ever. "It's…peaceful," she whispered, although it wasn't really peaceful. It was quiet. It was sad.

"Shh. Sleep," he said.

And what could she do but give him what he asked. It was all she *could* do. She knew she wouldn't sleep, but she tried, and eventually she slept. Because Shane's arms were around her.

Some time after that the stars disappeared behind a threatening cloud and Shane gathered up their things and gave Rachel a helmet with a light on it. He led them home.

"Don't go now," he said. "The roads are dark and deserted. You can have my room. I'll sleep in the spare."

She wanted him to hold her again, but he didn't. He simply walked away.

So she lay there in the dark, thinking about how she'd only made things worse for him by pushing. She'd forced him to face things he had put in a box. And now the scab had been removed from the wound and he was distant and unhappy.

Shane woke and got dressed the next morning feeling as if some of the heaviness he'd been carrying in his chest had been lifted and yet…it wasn't a pleasant feeling. Probably because he'd done what he hadn't wanted to do. In his urgency to give Rachel the truth he'd felt she deserved, he'd saddled her with more worry.

That wasn't right. There were a whole lot of things that weren't right. And it was no longer just about *his* pain now. He'd seen her face when he'd lost it last night. He'd dragged Rachel in. Down.

"Fix it, Merritt," he ordered. Yeah, and the first thing he was going to do was what should have already been done. The open house was in four days. Rachel had offered to let him off the hook and find a place to store the contents of Eric's room. But that wasn't fair or right.

Tension rose within him, hard and hot, as he thought of opening that door. But he beat it back.

Silently, he walked toward the room and turned the knob.

CHAPTER TEN

RACHEL felt the difference in the house when she woke up. There was a silence, a sense of anxiety, as if the whole world was just waiting to implode. As soon as she walked into the main part of the house she sensed what had happened, and her footsteps carried her to the room where Shane had buried his past.

The door was open. She didn't even have to be nosy or rude. And in the middle of the room, surrounded by boxes, by photo albums, by bits of paper and old souvenirs, Shane sat on a small sofa, the upholstery sagging.

He looked up when she came in, and she saw that he was holding a bundle of yellowing letters tied with a bedraggled pale peach ribbon.

"Are you...all right?" she whispered.

His response was to call her to his side. He brushed aside a pile of clothing, making a place for her. "I'm sorry about last night," he said.

"Sorry?"

"For hitting you with all that brutal stuff. For not—"

"Holding it in?" she said, standing up. "Shane, how can you say that? I'm so...honored that you agreed to tell me. I just hope I didn't push too hard."

To her surprise, he smiled slightly. "You always push. It's cute."

She blinked, unsure of how to react, but he took her hand and drew her to his side again. "You've spent so much time dealing with the detritus of this ranch. You deserve to see some of its history. Will you sit?"

She wedged in beside him, his warmth, the length of his thigh near hers, making her want to move closer. She resisted.

"It's all here, the pieces of their lives," Shane said. "Here's my mother's home in Boston. Here's Eric when he lost his two front teeth."

Rachel looked down at a photo of a very young smiling boy, clinging to the hand of his older brother, a much younger Shane. And the Shane in the photo was smiling back at Eric as they shared a private moment.

"He looked up to you," she said.

Shane shrugged. "He was a kid." Just as if Shane hadn't been "a kid," too. "Here's my mother's garden in better times." And now Rachel could see just how awesome a gardener Vera Merritt had been. The flowers were full and fat, purple and pink, white and gold blossoms a perfect contrast to the mountains in the distance and the green of the fields.

"She could have won prizes. She was an artist," she said.

"She would have liked to hear you say that. But..." He picked up the discarded letters. "These detail the events that led to my birth and to my mother marrying Frank. To her credit, she didn't lie to him or promise him anything. She was upfront about her reasons for marrying him. But it's clear that she wasn't happy. Unfortunately, Eric would have seen these after Frank died."

"He didn't know?" she asked incredulously.

"He was only four when she died. Why expose him to the dark stuff?"

"I don't care what you say. You were a good brother," she said, "and your mother must have loved you and your brother very much to make the kind of sacrifices she did. Mothers like that aren't born every day," she said, unable to keep the wistfulness out of her voice.

"Rachel, I wish—"

"No. My parents are imperfect, but they're mine and I'm fine with that. I'm okay," she said as he brushed his knuckles across her cheek. She couldn't help herself then. She leaned into his touch, but in her leaning her gaze fell on something.

"Shane, look at this," she said. She was staring down into a box, its contents a mess of papers. "These must be your brother's school papers." She picked up a handful and saw reports on "Calf Roping by the Numbers," "Alfalfa and Oats as Feed" and "The Road to Being a Quarterback."

"He wrote about what he loved," Shane said. "There's Eric right there in your hands." He took the papers, devouring the words as if now that he'd opened the doors and let the past in, he couldn't help himself.

"Shane." Rachel's heart nearly stopped.

He looked up. She held out a single sheet of paper. The title read, "Why My Brother is My Hero by Eric Merritt."

"I never knew he wrote that," Shane said.

"He wrote it after you left. Look at the date," she said.

When she turned to Shane he was staring at the ceiling. A single tear tracked down his cheek. Quietly, she got up and left him alone, closing the door behind her.

It felt as if this was already goodbye. Shane would be all right now, she hoped. He could be happy with his work, knowing that Eric had remembered the years when Shane had watched over him, cared for him and loved him.

Eric had just returned the favor. He'd given Shane a gift that was worth more than gold, silver and diamonds combined.

It was wonderful. They were a family again.

And she? She would soon be on her way elsewhere. Like always.

She was just about ready to go about her work when Shane came into the kitchen.

"I want to thank you," he said.

"For what?"

"For being in the road that day. I'm not sure I would have found that report if you hadn't been there. I might have burned everything."

"Shane…"

"Sorry. I can't seem to lie to you. That's why I'm not going to lie and tell you that some miracle has happened. It hasn't. I'm not eager to visit with the people of Moraine, but I'm going to."

"Because it's the right thing to do?"

"Because you want it so much."

Rachel felt a lump in her throat, and not a happy lump. To have Shane do something just because she wished it broke her heart. It touched her, but…

"You can't—"

He held up his hand to stop her. "And because even though I don't think I deserve forgiveness from my neighbors, I feel that they deserve the right to call the shots, not me. I'm not even sure how to approach them, though."

"Then you're lucky I've been thinking about this," she said, risking a smile.

His answering smile was the kind that was wide enough to reveal his dimples. "Why am I not surprised that you have a plan to get me to town?"

"Oh, not to town. Here. I was thinking…a gathering. Not the open house. That's four days away, anyway, and it's about business. This would be…I don't know… tomorrow. And just people."

"I wasn't thinking anything quite that formal. Or that soon."

"It doesn't have to be formal. Just all-inclusive. A party."

He looked a bit taken aback. "A party? Tomorrow? I don't see—"

"I'll make it happen."

"I don't want to put that kind of work on you."

"You won't be. I really do want this get-together, Shane. I'll be gone in four days. I'll never be a Moraine girl again, never a cowgirl again, never here with all of you again. They're nice people. You're nice people. Nice people should get together."

"And have parties?"

"Of course."

"Another rule to live by?"

"When you change schools every year or six months, you learn ways to get in quickly and connect with people, parties being one way. Because even if you never get to see them again, you still get to count them as friends."

"Damn it, Rachel."

Shane moved up beside her. He trailed his index

finger down her cheek. She felt the heat rise within her. She heard his breath quicken.

"I'm not going to kiss you this time. I promised that I wouldn't hurt you, but you…amaze me."

"I wish you would kiss me. And don't say 'Damn it, Rachel.' I know I'm being outrageous, but time is short."

"Kissing…accelerates things. Situations tend to get out of hand. At least that's how I know it's going to be with me if I kiss you."

She shook her head. "It won't. I won't let it."

He reached out and cupped her elbows, pulling her toward him. Their bodies weren't touching other than his fingertips feathering across her elbows. Then he leaned forward slowly and traced her lips with his tongue. Softly. Gently. He kissed her.

Her elbows tingled. Her lips tingled. Her…everything tingled. Heat rose within her. Higher. Higher still until she was swaying toward him. She was just going to wrap her arms around his neck, but she heard herself only seconds before, saying, "I won't let it." She remembered that Shane was the king of guilt. If something happened, he would not let her take the blame even if it was totally her fault.

And yet…she quickly looped one arm around his neck, kissed him quick, hard, drinking in as much of him as she could, tasting as much as she could manage. Then she squeezed her eyes tight and pushed away.

"You're safe," she said. And she didn't know whether she was talking to him or to herself.

"I don't feel safe," he said.

"Me, either," she admitted.

"How do you feel?"

Lost. So lost. She was losing him. Only four more days. Four short days and then a lifetime of no Shane.

Rachel took a deep breath. "I feel frustrated and as if I need to do a lot of stuff to take my mind off of kissing. Fortunately, I have a big party to plan." And, with that, she ran off to start planning.

Shane walked out onto the grassy area where Rachel and Marcia had hastily set up tables and chairs decorated with white tablecloths and Rachel's favorite flowers. He and Hank and Tom had constructed a makeshift wooden dance floor in record time. There would be musicians. There was food galore. "Some of which Marcia let me look at but not touch," Rachel had teased.

He had laughed. Hard to believe he had been able to laugh or look her in the face after all the things he had confessed the other night. He should be feeling self-conscious. He probably would be if the person on the receiving end had been anyone but Rachel.

Because Rachel wasn't like anyone else, he thought as he looked up to see her walking toward him. She was wearing her pretty blue-trimmed boots and a white fringed skirt with a blue blouse. A white hat hung down her back on a string, and she kept trying to look over her shoulder and see it, to no avail.

"Does any true cowgirl ever wear one of these?" she asked. "I'd hate for anyone to think I was making fun of real cowgirls."

He smiled at her because...he just couldn't help himself. "You can wear whatever you like. No one will mind."

And that theory was proven correct when the guests began arriving.

"Nice hat, Rachel," someone said.

"Beautiful, Rachel," a male voice said.

Shane swung around to see Jarrod Ollis staring him in the eyes.

"Want to fight over her?" Jarrod teased. "I'll wrestle you for her."

"Are you actually trying to manipulate me into a fight?" Shane asked with a smile. "If I recall—and I do—the last time we fought, you walked away with a broken arm."

"A scratch."

It had been much more than a scratch, and it hadn't been a good-natured fight that time, either. Shane took a deep breath. "I'm—Jarrod, I'm sorry."

"About the broken arm? Forget it. I was probably asking for it."

He hadn't been. Not really. "About the arm, but also…about everything." That covered a lot of territory. He wanted to be more specific, but when he opened his mouth to speak, Jarrod punched him in the arm. Gently.

"Hey, man, no. I didn't come here to humiliate you or for an apology. Lots of things happened. We were young and stupid, then not so young. Maybe still stupid at times. Whatever. Things change. Some bad things happened to both of us. Probably to all of us. But I'm still here. And so are you. I came to see you."

Shane's chest felt tight. He could see Rachel over Jarrod's shoulder. She was fanning her face as if trying not to cry. So, for her sake, he couldn't lose it right here. But he slapped Jarrod on the back. "I'm glad you're here," he said.

By then the guests had started arriving fast and furious. Ruby and Angie and Cynthia cornered him.

"We missed you, you big...Shane," Angie said.

"Come into the store anytime," Cynthia offered. "I'll pull out your favorite licorice whips."

"I'll be sure to come by the store and the diner before I go," he promised. And then... "I've missed you," he said, and meant it as he gave them each a big hug.

"Don't think you're going to get away with one hug from me," Ruby warned. "I want two hugs and a kiss on the cheek."

"I can do better than that," Shane said, meeting her demands and then swinging her around in a circle.

"Shane," she shrieked. "Put me down. I weigh a ton."

"You're a feather," he told her.

She laughed. "Oh, I've missed you more than you can ever imagine."

And that was when he lost it. He pulled Ruby close and hugged her again. "I'm sorry, so sorry for holding you at arm's length. You mothered me a lot when I was growing up. Even when I was bad."

"You don't ever have to apologize to me," she said. "But I'm so glad to see you again. I owe Rachel a lot."

"I owe her more."

"You're really going to let her get away?"

"Ruby..."

"All right, I won't pry."

"You'd better have a good time, though," he warned. "Rachel worked like the dickens to pull this off. I want it to be the best night ever."

Because after this...the open house didn't really count. There would be lots of people. The ads had gone out, complete with Rachel's photos, to five counties. He might not get to see her alone for more than a minute or two that day. They had reached the top of the mountain and now they were rushing to the bottom. Shane took a deep breath and dived into Rachel's party.

At some point he took the mike and thanked everyone for coming. Despite Jarrod's words, Shane told everyone he was sorry he had been rude and distant and in general a jerk, and was shushed by the crowd. But he saw a damp eye or two or three, and some sad faces when he finished thanking them for loving his baby brother and for being good neighbors to Eric in his absence, so he was glad he'd been allowed to apologize.

And then he found himself searching out Rachel. As if she knew he'd been looking for her, she came to him. The band was tuning up their fiddles and mandolins and banjos. And then they began to play.

She grinned and mimed dancing with him.

He took her hand, even though what he really wanted was just to walk with her, talk with her, be with her.

Rachel walked right into his arms. "I'm not the best dancer," she confessed.

It didn't matter. He would have her in his arms.

"I'll muffle my screams of pain if you step on my toes," he promised.

She hit him, lightly, and that was good. Because while he was teasing her, and she was reacting, he couldn't do what he really wanted to. Which was to kiss her crazy.

Dancing with Rachel was torture. Exquisite torture. And over too soon.

Everything with Rachel would be over too soon. And he would have to smile through his pain. Because she was following her dreams.

* * *

Rachel couldn't stop humming even after the last guest had gone home. The evening had been magical, and she didn't want it to end. Even though she knew it was already over. And tomorrow…tomorrow…

"One more," Shane whispered, coming up behind her and taking her in his arms as he swung her into a dance, just as if the party was still going on.

Except it wasn't. They were at the ranch, they were alone and she was so in love with him that she couldn't think straight. She was in deepest danger of doing something stupid, showing her hand. She had to lighten things up.

"So…what do you think? Ruby and Len? Maybe an item?" she asked.

Shane tilted back his head and laughed. "She was beating him over the head when he stepped on her foot. He was hopping around like a bunny that had lost its sense of direction. And the dog…the dog…"

They stopped dancing. They laughed, holding each other. "The dog…" Shane said. "I thought the dog was going to be trampled between them. I don't know if Otter was trying to save Len from Ruby's blows or if he just wanted to dance with them. Good thing you got in there and saved him. You're as good with animals as you are with children, Rachel."

"He looked as if he needed a friend," she said.

And that was when the laughter stopped.

"You've been just what I needed, what everyone in Moraine needed. You made this happen," Shane said. "This whole wonderful evening was your doing."

"No," she said quietly. "No, it wasn't. You made them happy, Shane."

"They made me happy. And this night…it was time. You were right. All along. Maine doesn't know just how lucky a state it is," he whispered fiercely. While he was talking, he was slowly walking her up against a wall. He took her hands in his.

"I'm not sure a state can be considered lucky," she said, a trifle breathlessly.

He lifted her hands and placed them against the wall on either side of her head, his palms holding her there gently as he nudged her head to one side with his nose and kissed right beneath her earlobe.

She melted.

"Lucky. Like me. I feel lucky to have you with me tonight," he said.

His lips slid down to the curve of her neck. To her shoulder.

She shivered and his eyes turned molten. He released her as his lips met hers. He gathered her to him and slid his hands over her shoulders, just beneath the curve of her breast...

The sound of Hank closing a gate somewhere in the distance registered. He wasn't close. He wouldn't come to the house. But Shane backed away. "I promised I wouldn't do this," he told her. "I shouldn't have started it."

"Not smart of either of us," she agreed. "But...you didn't want it?"

He looked at her with astonishment. "Do I look like I'm insane and unaware of how desirable you are?"

"No one's ever told me that before, that I'm desirable."

Shane growled. "Then the men you've known must have been wearing their heads on backward, because you are the most desirable woman I know," he said as his hand snaked around her waist. He slammed her up against him. He kissed her hard, his body molded to hers. Every inch of her body was curved against his. "Bodies don't lie, so don't lie to yourself. If it weren't for Hank reminding me that it would be a major mistake for us to sleep together, I would be begging you to come to my bed."

She looped an arm around his neck. "All right. You win. I'm what you wanted tonight." Then she smiled up at him sadly. She kissed him, just once. Somehow—she didn't know how—she managed to back away, because backing away was the only choice when so much was at risk.

In only a second she would be far enough away to break the spell of being near him. She hoped.

But then she made the mistake of looking directly into his eyes, and that always messed with her common sense. "You wouldn't have had to beg me to come to your bed. I was already there in my mind," she confessed. "Thank goodness one of us thought things through, or we would have been naked together and regretting it ever afterward."

And then she turned and ran for her car.

"Idiot. Fool. What's wrong with you?" she whispered as she began to drive home, just a bit too fast. But that answer was already obvious. She was in love with Shane.

And her heart was already preparing itself for the pain to come. Because, no matter what milestones he had passed tonight, he was still going. Mending fences didn't negate the fact that he loved his work. He loved moving around. He didn't want a relationship.

If she were very smart—and she had once thought that she was—she would start putting on the emotional brakes. She could pull away right now, just get on a bus and ride away. She had enough money now, and not going was going to land her in major hurt territory. There would be broken pieces of her that might not go back together again. There would be substantial scarring of her heart, the kind that never disappeared.

Still...not staying would leave Shane alone to face that open house and the auction, selling off the house where his mother and brother had lived and died.

"So suck it up, Everly. You know you're not leaving him until it's all done and he's back on his way to happy." Still, she had to be very careful. Who knew what foolish things she might do between now and then?

CHAPTER ELEVEN

Rachel and Shane sat on the porch beneath a star-filled sky. *Last time to do this,* she thought. The house was finished. Tomorrow was the sale. But she didn't want to think about that.

"They're so beautiful. There are so many of them," she said.

"I meant for you to have a chance to enjoy them that night we camped out. I'm sorry you didn't get the chance."

"I'm seeing them now. I suppose some people would find this mundane, but I've never really spent much time looking at stars. Most of the places I've lived have too much light pollution to see more than a few of the brightest ones."

"My mother used to tell Eric and me that stars were a giant's dandruff. Mostly, I think, because Eric had this amazingly contagious laughter. We used to think up things to make him laugh just to hear it."

She smiled. "What a nice memory."

"I'd almost forgotten it."

"I'm glad you didn't. Remembering your brother's laughter is a good thing, isn't it?"

"It was one of the best things about him. Are you sure you're not cold? It's a bit chilly tonight."

She sighed and leaned back against the porch support. "I'm…just right. In fact, I could fall asleep right here in this very spot. Did you ever do that?"

"Sleep on the porch? Lots of times. Lots of mosquito bites in the morning." He flicked an imaginary one away from her nose.

She leaned toward him, following his touch. "Shane, do you think we've done enough? I want tomorrow to be perfect," she said. "Lots of people coming to look at your house. I want it to shine like silver. Nothing left undone."

He laughed. "You've checked and double checked everything."

"As if you didn't," she teased.

"Yeah, but that's what I do. I'm a numbers man, a checklist kind of guy."

"And I'm a 'try to make everything right' woman."

"Do you seriously want to look one more time?"

No. She seriously wanted him to lean closer and kiss her. She wanted them to slide to the porch wrapped in each other's arms. She wanted to plunge her fingers into Shane's thick, dark hair. And because she wanted those things so badly…

"I think one more look around wouldn't hurt." She got to her feet.

He groaned, but then he laughed. "The royal tour, then?"

"Nothing but the best for us."

So they opened the door and stared at the wonders they had created. The living room was perfect. "I still love that green vase, even in lamplight," she said. "Maybe especially in lamplight. I hope someone gives you bundles of money for it."

They moved to the kitchen, redone in sunshine

yellow and turquoise, with black and white tile on the floor. "If anyone makes one remark about tearing this place down, don't tell me. This room is perfect as it is."

The tour continued. The dining room, the enclosed porch. Finally they came to Eric's room. Rachel had come in early and she and Shane had worked as long as they could.

"You were right about the very subtle cowboy theme, the hat on the shelf, the boots in the corner," he said. "I thought it might be tacky, but done up in rust and brown and gold this place is Eric through and through. And I'm glad. It feels warm. It feels complete."

"Thank you," she said softly. "I tried not to change too much. And now...I guess there's nowhere else to go, no more rooms to inspect. Everything is in its place."

"Tomorrow we let the masses give it a yes vote or a no vote, I suppose."

"They wouldn't dare give it a no vote," she said, making him laugh. She laughed, too, but there were tears in her heart. Because when tomorrow was over Shane would turn over anything that hadn't sold to a company that would continue the sale online. And then she would leave him.

"And then we'll both leave," he said. "You'll go to Maine."

"You'll go to Germany."

"I'd like to know that you're all right," he said.

Her heart stalled. She'd experienced so many endings, but this one...she couldn't drag out her goodbyes. Her heart was ripping in half already. "I'll—I'll send you a postcard," she said.

He froze. "Damn you, Rachel. That's cold."

"Said the boy who was born to break hearts."

"Not yours. I don't want to break yours. Not that I could, but…I don't want…"

"*I* want," she said suddenly.

This whole situation, this polite farewell. Everything was so clean, so neat, so dry, so terrible. And she had always been a messy person.

"I want a souvenir," she said. "Just one thing." She wrapped her arms around his neck and kissed him.

He kissed her back. Fervently. And then…more fervently.

"I don't want to forget you," she whispered.

"I want you to forget me," he said. "I don't want to be a regret for you."

"You won't. You'll be a memory. A great memory. The kind I couldn't possibly forget."

"That's what I want, too," he said. "Wait here." And he took off as if the house was on fire.

In a few seconds she heard the sound of banging and clanging. She started toward the bedroom.

"Don't come in here," he warned. "In fact, go into the living room and close the door."

"I don't think—"

"Good. I don't want you to think right now. Just feel." And then he was gone again. Ten minutes later he came to get her. His hair was disheveled. His shirt was half untucked. "Come on, my little astronomer."

"Astronomer?"

"You wanted to sleep beneath the stars. Well, I can't promise you sleep, but I can promise you something better than the porch." He led her out of the house into the yard, and there beside the garden, with the fragrance of night roses wafting over them, was a bed fully assembled.

"We're having a sleepover?" she asked, and her heart started pounding.

"I hadn't gotten that far yet. I just wanted you to finally have your wish, your souvenir. A night beneath Montana skies."

He held a hand out toward the bed, and she saw that he had piled up pillows. A person could lie back and easily, comfortably look up at the heavens. If looking up was what they wanted to do.

"I can see now what all those women saw, why so many of them cried when you left. You're a master of the gallant gesture."

He chuckled as he sat on the side of the bed, took her hand and drew her down beside him. "Believe me, this is a first for me. Beds aren't made to be dragged out into the night."

"But you did it. Thank you. It was a heroic effort, and I—"

"Rachel?"

She looked up at him. He smiled down at her.

"Shh," he said, and he slipped his hands into her hair and kissed her.

He drew her down so that they were lying on the bed. And he kissed her some more. Deeply. His mouth driving her slowly crazy, his hands wandering over her body, slipping beneath her blouse, leaving trails of fire burning within her.

She clutched at him, unbuttoned his shirt with more speed than skill, popping a button as she revealed his chest. She slid her palms up over his naked skin and loved the sound of his breath catching in his throat.

"Rachel," he said on a groan.

"Yes."

"No. I shouldn't have started this. We're not doing

this." He reached out and began to rearrange her clothing where he had left her skin exposed.

Her heart went cold, like a rock in winter. "We're not?"

"No. And not because I'm not dying to. I'm burning up for you. My hands are shaking with the need to touch you. But tomorrow..."

"Tomorrow it ends."

"I want it to end right for you. With no regrets. I don't want you to hate me afterward."

She would never hate him. But the fact that he cared... She leaned forward and kissed him on the chest. He visibly swallowed. His breathing became more shallow.

"And I also don't want you to have to worry about falling asleep and having Hank find us this way," he said in a raspy voice.

She shrieked. "Hank? I hadn't even thought of Hank."

"Neither had I when I came up with the not so bright idea of dragging the bed out here. Still, Hank isn't the main reason we're just going to lie here and stare at the stars while I hold you. I want...I want you to be different. I don't want you to be the topic of gossip. You're so strong and beautiful and proud. I would hate to have anyone use that sympathetic, sorrowful tone when they talked about you."

"Shane, that's so...nice." But she didn't think she could bear it if he didn't at least kiss her some more. She placed her palm low on his stomach and leaned closer.

A shudder ripped through his body. He placed his hand over hers, stopping her. "Damn it, Rachel. For once I'm trying to do the right thing, and I'm not sure

I've ever done anything that tested me so much in my life. Now…the stars…please."

She gave a tight nod, kissed his arm and lay back in his arms. "Show me your stars, Shane." He was trying to make her different from all his other women. Despite the pain in her heart, the knowledge that she would never spend a night in his arms, Rachel intended to help him do—or not do—this thing.

So she lay beside him as they whispered about the constellations and he showed her the sky he'd grown up with. He showed her Sagittarius and Hercules and Corona Borealis. As he spoke, his deep voice echoed through her body. His left arm tightened around her as he pointed out the stars with his right. Gradually, she began to relax, to appreciate the beauty and the wonder of simply lying here with him, sharing this with him.

She felt…special…and as his voice died away she looked up at him to tell him so.

He smiled down at her, and then a curse word left his lips. Rachel blinked, then learned the reason why as fast-moving clouds started blotting out some of the stars and a few drops of rain fell on her face.

Without even talking, they leaped from the bed. Rachel grabbed the bedding, Shane muscled the mattress up on the porch, then came back for the frame. By the time they were done the clouds had obliterated all of the stars and both of them were wearing wet clothes.

"I can't believe I did that to you," he said, but he was laughing. "I can't believe I didn't know there was rain in the forecast."

"Well, you're a numbers man, not a weatherman," she told him, laughing up at him. "Shane?"

He looked at her.

"I'm really wet. I'm going inside to take my clothes off."

"Rachel?"

"Yes."

"I'm going to follow you, and I hope you'll understand when I tell you that I think I used up my last drop of willpower back in that bed. If you take your clothes off, I'm going to want to look."

"I'm so glad to hear that." She didn't even wait to get inside. She shucked her boots, pulled her blouse over her head and tossed it aside, then removed her pants until all that remained was her candy-apple-red bra and panties.

Shane came at her like a madman, wrapping her in his arms, crushing her to him and kissing her crazy. "Tell me to stop," he told her. "I'm not even close to being in control."

"Don't stop," she begged. "I love all your fancy constellation talk, but…don't stop." She rose on her toes. She kissed whatever parts of him she could reach.

Somewhere along the line his shirt and pants and… everything came off. He removed the remaining scraps of red silk from her body and dropped with her onto the bare mattress lying on the porch.

They kissed, they clutched and finally they created some new constellations of their own as the rain came down and the darkness enfolded them. He loved her long and well throughout the night. And as the sun came up he kissed her throat.

He stared down at her, a worried look in his beautiful blue eyes. "I don't want you to ever be sorry for this, to regret this summer," he told her.

She tried out a shaky smile. Because she knew that what he was asking her just wasn't completely possible.

She would love him forever. She would regret the pain that would follow her all her days. Still, this…

"This was wonderful," she told him. "Thank you for everything." And that was all she was going to say.

He didn't look happy.

She didn't feel happy. Because the night was over. The auction was today. The words "the end" loomed large in her mind.

When she came out of the shower, where she had retreated, she knew that something was wrong. Different. Shane was staring at the phone.

She moved to his side.

"I've already had an offer on the ranch. On everything in it. A group of local investors saw it on the internet, pooled their funds and want the whole thing. Now. No auction."

His voice sounded… She didn't know how it sounded. Her heart had fallen out of her body, or maybe it was simply being squeezed by a giant fist, because all she could think was, *It's over. Too soon. This is goodbye, the last conversation, the last anything.* She wasn't even sure she could speak without her voice catching. And if she didn't speak he would know just how much she was hurting. That would hurt *him*. Again. It just wasn't happening. She wasn't letting it.

Rachel cleared her throat. "Are you accepting the offer?"

He looked at her, but she couldn't read his expression. "It's what I came to do."

She nodded, even tried a smile. "All right. Good. That will save you a lot of trouble. Do you need me to…?"

She looked around, trying to seem cheerful. Here

was where he'd kissed her. There was the vase she loved, Cynthia's curtains, the rooms Shane had walked in and grown up in and where she'd learned to love him heart and soul. It was going, going, gone…and not even an auction in sight.

"I think…we should both leave today," he said. "Now. It's what we planned, anyway. Just earlier than expected. I'll make some calls, take you to the airport, get you on an early flight and…"

"No." She touched his hand. "Don't drive me." She couldn't bear a public goodbye at an airport. "I'll leave now. Hank can pick up the car. Ruby will make sure I have transportation. I think this is the way we should end. Here at the ranch. Maybe…this minute." Because if they didn't end right now, she was surely going to let her tears fall.

"If you like."

No. There was no *like* about it. She wanted the impossible. She wanted Shane. However she could have him. She had become one of those women Ruby comforted.

Without another second of hesitation, Rachel looped one arm around his neck and kissed him quickly. "This was the best summer ever," she said fiercely. "Kiss Lizzie goodbye for me and give her some extra oats. Make sure the new people aren't mean to her. And—"

"Rachel—" Shane's voice broke. He pulled her hard against his chest and his lips met hers. She leaned into him as tears threatened.

Just a few seconds more, she pleaded. *Don't cry now. Don't, Rachel.* She ran for the car, climbed in and hit the gas. Shane disappeared from her rearview mirror.

And the tears fell.

* * *

Shane kicked the wall. He kicked a few other things, too. She was gone. Gone forever. And the look in her eyes...

Something was wrong. And he was pretty sure that he knew what it was. Rachel wasn't a jump-into-bed kind of woman. She wouldn't do that lightly. But when that call had come this morning it had caught him by surprise. So much so that the sense of loss at ending things so quickly and finally had hit him sledgehammer hard, and he had just wanted to get past it. He'd been callous in his suggestion that they end it now. Hell, he hadn't said any of the things he'd wanted to say. Things like, *Thank you for being you, thank you for bringing light into my life, thank you for saving me from myself.*

And then there had been all the things he never *could* say. Things like, *I love you. I love you. I love you.*

He kicked the bedpost, the one he had still not put back together, and it fell over with a bang.

She was gone. *Get used to it, Merritt.*

But that was never going to happen. Slowly, he began to gather his things, getting ready to leave. Rachel would soon be living her dream life, and he owed it to her not to be a pathetic lovesick guy. He could never call her. If he did, she would know something was wrong and she would worry.

He just couldn't do that to her. And yet...something was flat out wrong ending things this way. She'd had so many aborted stays in her life, being dragged here and there with no fanfare at all. And here was another aborted ending.

Just once in her life she should have a joyful farewell, with people saying all the right things.

"She's already gone," he said. "It's too late."

Yes. Most people would think that way. But Rachel had never been like most people, and she had taught him a thing or two.

He picked up the telephone.

Rachel couldn't figure out what was wrong with Ruby. The woman wasn't herself at all.

"I'll see about getting you a ride, but I think there may be some problem at the airport. I heard something on the news earlier. This could take a while," Ruby said.

"What kind of problem?"

"Oh, I don't know. Some holdup. Planes stacked in. They're telling people not to show up yet."

Rachel raised an eyebrow. "Maybe I should call and get an update."

"Oh. No. There are lots of flights today. You need some breakfast. You didn't even eat breakfast."

She hadn't, but...

"How do you know that?"

"I just...I think I know you a little bit by now, Rachel Everly. I just know it. Are you calling me a liar?"

Rachel didn't have time to say no. The phone rang, and Ruby jumped up and ran into the next room to answer it. "Sorry, got to take this. A businesswoman has to always be available, you know."

Apparently there was a lot of business today. The phone kept ringing. Ruby kept talking in low, fervent whispers. Was she having problems with her business? Rachel would make sure that Ruby at least was okay before she left today.

The thought made Rachel sad. So many friends

she would never see again, never know what had happened to them. An image of Shane reared up in her consciousness. Rachel closed her eyes.

"Honey, are you sure you're all right?"

She opened her eyes to find Ruby frowning down at her.

Lie. Lie, she told herself. *What purpose would it serve to worry your friend?* "I'm just fine," she tried to say, but her voice came out garbled and thick. "I really need to leave," she finally managed. "I have to call the airport, and if there's a problem there call Shane and let him know." She couldn't get trapped in an airport with him. Not after she'd managed to make it this far without letting him see that she'd been stupid enough to love a man who had told her from day one that he couldn't love, couldn't promise.

"Sweetie, he knows," Ruby said, and she enfolded Rachel in her arms.

Panic erupted in Rachel like a volcano. "He knows what?" That she loved him? No, no, no. Don't let him know that.

Ruby looked panicked, as if she'd made a mistake herself. "He knows about the airport, I'm sure. He has people to do those things for him, and I'm—I think—"

The sound of sirens blaring interrupted her. Both women looked up. There was yelling, screaming, something that sounded like a drum and a fiddle and—

Rachel raced Ruby to the window.

"Thank goodness. I thought I was going to have to tie you down," Ruby said. "Come on, sweetie. Shane knows you need something better than a handshake and a peck on the cheek goodbye."

Fear gripped Rachel's heart. "I don't understand."

"You will. Come on."

A part of Rachel wanted to dig in her heels. She was pretty darn sure that if this had something to do with Shane she should back away. If she saw him again, or had to talk about him to anyone, she was definitely going to make a fool of herself. But the part of her that was desperately, pathetically in love with him didn't have the strength to run away again. She followed Ruby out onto the lawn of the boarding house.

A group of people had gathered there. Len and some men were in the back of a pickup truck with musical instruments.

"Have to have music at a going away party," he said, smiling and tipping his hat to her as they began to play some soft, lonely tune that pulled at Rachel's heart.

Other people held homemade signs that read, "We'll miss you, Rachel," and "Good luck in Maine," and "Don't forget us, Rachel." Some of the signs had been painted, and the paint was clearly still wet.

"Rachel, we wish we'd had more time, but we brought food. You can't say goodbye without cake," Angie said, and she and Cynthia and some of the other men and women began to set out folding tables and chairs and bring out food.

There was chatter, and people began to hug her. She hugged them back, thanked them and turned to Ruby. "You did this so fast!" A lump nearly choked her, but she got the words out and hugged her friend, kissing her cheek.

"Not me," Ruby said. "I told you. I'm thrilled this is happening, but this was all Shane."

But Shane wasn't here. Rachel knew then that he had wanted her to have a goodbye party, but they had already said their goodbyes. She tried to accept that and smile at her friends. They had gone to so much trouble for her.

There were even games of several types, and someone gave Rachel a horseshoe. When she turned to throw it in the wrong direction a cry rang out. "I'm just getting my bearings," she said, a bit sheepishly. "I wasn't going to throw it yet."

But apparently it wasn't her lack of skill with a horseshoe that was causing the uproar. People were pointing and calling out Shane's name, and Rachel looked up to see him flying down the road in his pickup truck, the dust curling in a low cloud behind him.

Her heart began to thump wildly, erratically. Her throat felt thick with tears. For the first time in her life she thought she might actually faint. Somehow she didn't.

Shane drove close to the crowd, jumped out of the truck and walked right up to her. "Hello again, sunshine. I'm sorry. I know you wanted it to be a short goodbye, but...I just couldn't do it. It had to be right. You need to know how important you are, how much you'll be missed, that this wasn't just an ordinary summer. It was different, better. It was special because of you."

Oh, no. The first teardrop slipped down her cheek. She just couldn't stop it.

"Don't," Shane whispered. "I didn't mean to hurt you." He stepped forward, took a handkerchief out of his pocket and wiped the tear away gently.

"They're tears of joy," she said, and that was partly true and partly very much a lie. "Thank you. For this." She gestured to the crowd. *This* was so wonderful. People had obviously stopped their busy lives to make this happen for her. She was not going to ruin it for them by crying. If only she could stop.

"She's crying." Jarrod stated the obvious. "I— Rachel, I think those are presents Shane has in his truck."

That Jarrod was trying so hard to cheer her up only made the tears flow faster. She swiped them away.

The crowd turned to look at the back of the truck, which appeared to be crammed full. There was a log cabin quilt covering whatever was inside. "I'm sorry I didn't have time to do this right," Shane said. "You should have had everything wrapped in gold ribbons and silver star paper. This isn't all I hoped it would be."

She looked at him, hoping her heart wasn't in her eyes. "I don't need silver paper. But I don't understand. What are you giving me?"

"A home. Or at least some of the things from the ranch you've grown to treasure." He handed her the green glass vase that had gotten her eyes glowing so many times, her favorite mug, a small and exquisite oak table. Slowly he revealed the secrets beneath the quilt.

"Not your mother's favorite china? Shane, I love it. You know that. But you can't give that to me."

"Why not? You're building a dream life. You'll need things, and you should have things you love."

"But they're yours."

"And I was going to sell them," he said. "You treasured them the way I should have."

Suddenly, something wasn't right. "You said the buyers wanted the house and all its contents. Shane, you can't do that. You can't let me have these things. That would be stealing."

His fierce, steady gaze suddenly flickered. "No, it wouldn't. I—I decided not to sell the ranch."

"Just like that?"

"Quicker than that."

"Why?"

"I'd rather not say."

She shook her head. "But Shane—"

"Because that house *is* a home now. It wasn't before you came. You loved it up and changed it. You changed *me*. And now…things are different."

"Will you rent it out?"

He took her hands. "It doesn't matter, does it? What matters is that you're going to have what you want and need. I'm glad of that. But I want you to know, if you ever pass this way again, we'll be here for you. You have family here. You have a permanent place to come to."

"You're staying?" The words came out on a whisper, on a breath.

"I don't think I can do anything other than stay. You made me see the ranch through your eyes. You taught me to let people in, not shut them out. This place feels like family now. It's where I belong."

She bit her lip. She nodded. "I'm glad."

As if no one else but the two of them were there, he cupped her face with his palms. "I want you to be happy. Supremely happy. To have all the things you've ever dreamed of."

But of course that was no longer possible. She gazed up at him with her heart in her eyes.

"What if my dream changes? What if I've realized that a home isn't one never-changing place?"

"Rachel." He said her name on a breath. Somewhere someone sighed. "What are you saying?"

She set down the vase she was still holding. "All those other times when I had to leave a place I didn't fight back. I went because there was no one on my side, no one I could trust. But…I trust you. You've opened up my world, inspired me to take risks and make better choices. I'd like to make one of those choices right now."

"Do it," he said. "If it's that you don't want my mother's dishes, I can find you something you'll like better."

She bopped him on the arm. "I love your mother's dishes. I don't want to talk about dishes. I want to talk about you. About me. About how I want to stay here and how I don't want to be another woman who ends up crying on Ruby's bosom. I want you to love me, but if you can't—"

Rachel never got the chance to say the words. Shane tugged her to him and she tumbled into his arms. "I've been in love with you for weeks." His voice was a fierce, dark whisper.

"And you didn't tell me?"

"You had things to do. In Maine. Without me. I wanted you to have your dream."

"You *are* my dream. Every night. Every day."

"Good," he said. "Because I'm never leaving you. Not now. Not ever."

"Can you afford to keep the ranch?"

"If I want to, I can afford never to work again in my life. I'm rich, Rachel, but I think I'd like to ranch even though I'm not a cattleman. I'll be a horse rancher."

"And I'll be a horse rancher's wife. If you'll have me."

Shane laughed out loud. He kissed her hard. "That's

my beautiful, exciting, exhilarating Rachel. Impatient. Mouthy."

"Shane, you didn't answer my question. Everyone is waiting. I'm—I confess that I'm a little nervous. I didn't mean to blurt that out."

And then her wonderful rancher went down on one knee. "I'll have you. I'd never have any other. And I'll love you until the stars turn their lights out."

"Shane, there's still something in that truck, isn't there?" Jarrod asked. "Something big. What is it?"

"It's a secret," he said. "It's just for Rachel."

She looked at him with a question in her eyes, but she was willing to wait for the answer. She had what she wanted, after all. Her rancher.

"I always knew he was a rancher," Ruby said, and everyone laughed. "More importantly, I knew he was Rachel's rancher. She flipped him over and found all the hidden parts none of us had ever looked for. She found his heart."

"And she owns it," Shane whispered against Rachel's hair. "I don't need to move around anymore. There's no longer anything to run from, and what I've spent my life searching for is right here."

Hours later, as they pulled up at the ranch and climbed out of the truck, Rachel started to go inside.

"I'll be right there," Shane said. "There's something in the truck that we need."

"Dishes?" she asked. "Shane, I don't think so. We've been eating all afternoon."

"I know, and I'm not hungry for food. But we might need a bed. It's in here somewhere."

Rachel shrieked. She ran to him and put her arms around his waist. "You were giving me your bed? The one we made love on?"

"It wasn't my bed, it was ours after that," he said stubbornly. "I kept the pillows that still carry the scent of your perfume and gave you the rest. I wanted to feel that you were with me when I slept. I wanted you to remember the man who loved you on that bed. It was selfish, I guess. A better man wouldn't have tried to remind you of our last night together."

She slid in front of him, rose on her toes and kissed him. "There isn't a better man than you, Shane."

"I hope you always feel that way," he said. And he lifted her into his arms and started toward the barn.

"Shane, where are you taking me? What about the bed?"

"I'll get to that in just a minute, my love," he said. "For now I'm taking you to tell the kids that their mother's home. And this time she's staying forever. She's ours."

Rachel laughed. "I do love Lizzie and Rambler and all the others," she said.

"And I love you, Rachel. No more endings. No more moving. Just you and me, beginning the rest of our life together. Every single morning."

EPILOGUE

Two weeks later, Rachel walked across the grass near the creek at Oak Valley. She was dressed all in white, her long veil flowing out behind her.

And waiting for her beside the creek was her cowboy.

She reached him and he pulled her straight into his arms, kissed her long and slow and sweet.

The minister cleared his throat.

"Sorry," Shane said, "but I waited a long time to come back to Oak Valley. Too long. I don't want to wait for the good stuff anymore."

"Well, you'll wait for this woman if you want to wed her," the minister ordered.

"In that case, I'll wait forever," he said, backing away as Rachel rushed forward and launched into his arms.

The minister rolled his eyes.

"You might as well give up for a while. Once they start kissing, it tends to go on and on," someone said.

But Shane and Rachel heard, and both of them stepped away. "We like to kiss," Rachel said, "but we want to get married."

"We're *going* to get married," Shane said. "Today."

"And then they're going to be so happy," Ruby said.

"Rachel is going to college here, and she's going to be a teacher and our local photographer. Shane is going to be a rancher."

"I thought that Shane hated ranching," someone called out.

"He only thought he did. Until he looked at it through Rachel's eyes."

The conversation was going on all around Shane and Rachel until someone said, "Shh."

Shane was very quietly saying his vows. For Rachel's ears alone. "I promise to love you," he ended, repeating the words he'd already said.

"I promise to adore you," Rachel added.

"I promise to…" He leaned over and whispered in her ear. She turned a delicious shade of pink.

"Now?"

"Tonight," Shane promised.

"I now pronounce you man and wife," the minister said, rushing in. "You may kiss the bride."

But he already was. And as he tipped his bride back and her skirts rode up, the toes of a pair of boots with blue trim peeped out.

"Am I a real cowgirl now?" she asked her husband.

"You're *my* cowgirl now."

"That's the very best kind. And you're my cowboy."

"Right from the start, sweetheart. And to the end of time."

SEPTEMBER 2011
HARDBACK TITLES

ROMANCE

The Kanellis Scandal	Michelle Reid
Monarch of the Sands	Sharon Kendrick
One Night in the Orient	Robyn Donald
His Poor Little Rich Girl	Melanie Milburne
The Sultan's Choice	Abby Green
The Return of the Stranger	Kate Walker
Girl in the Bedouin Tent	Annie West
Once Touched, Never Forgotten	Natasha Tate
Nice Girls Finish Last	Natalie Anderson
The Italian Next Door...	Anna Cleary
From Daredevil to Devoted Daddy	Barbara McMahon
Little Cowgirl Needs a Mum	Patricia Thayer
To Wed a Rancher	Myrna Mackenzie
Once Upon a Time in Tarrula	Jennie Adams
The Secret Princess	Jessica Hart
Blind Date Rivals	Nina Harrington
Cort Mason – Dr Delectable	Carol Marinelli
Survival Guide to Dating Your Boss	Fiona McArthur

HISTORICAL

The Lady Gambles	Carole Mortimer
Lady Rosabella's Ruse	Ann Lethbridge
The Viscount's Scandalous Return	Anne Ashley
The Viking's Touch	Joanna Fulford

MEDICAL ROMANCE™

Return of the Maverick	Sue MacKay
It Started with a Pregnancy	Scarlet Wilson
Italian Doctor, No Strings Attached	Kate Hardy
Miracle Times Two	Josie Metcalfe

0811 Gen Std LP

SEPTEMBER 2011
LARGE PRINT TITLES

ROMANCE

Too Proud to be Bought	Sharon Kendrick
A Dark Sicilian Secret	Jane Porter
Prince of Scandal	Annie West
The Beautiful Widow	Helen Brooks
Rancher's Twins: Mum Needed	Barbara Hannay
The Baby Project	Susan Meier
Second Chance Baby	Susan Meier
Her Moment in the Spotlight	Nina Harrington

HISTORICAL

More Than a Mistress	Ann Lethbridge
The Return of Lord Conistone	Lucy Ashford
Sir Ashley's Mettlesome Match	Mary Nichols
The Conqueror's Lady	Terri Brisbin

MEDICAL ROMANCE™

Summer Seaside Wedding	Abigail Gordon
Reunited: A Miracle Marriage	Judy Campbell
The Man with the Locked Away Heart	Melanie Milburne
Socialite...or Nurse in a Million?	Molly Evans
St Piran's: The Brooding Heart Surgeon	Alison Roberts
Playboy Doctor to Doting Dad	Sue MacKay

ROMANCE

The Most Coveted Prize	Penny Jordan
The Costarella Conquest	Emma Darcy
The Night that Changed Everything	Anne McAllister
Craving the Forbidden	India Grey
The Lost Wife	Maggie Cox
Heiress Behind the Headlines	Caitlin Crews
Weight of the Crown	Christina Hollis
Innocent in the Ivory Tower	Lucy Ellis
Flirting With Intent	Kelly Hunter
A Moment on the Lips	Kate Hardy
Her Italian Soldier	Rebecca Winters
The Lonesome Rancher	Patricia Thayer
Nikki and the Lone Wolf	Marion Lennox
Mardie and the City Surgeon	Marion Lennox
Bridesmaid Says, 'I Do!'	Barbara Hannay
The Princess Test	Shirley Jump
Breaking Her No-Dates Rule	Emily Forbes
Waking Up With Dr Off-Limits	Amy Andrews

HISTORICAL

The Lady Forfeits	Carole Mortimer
Valiant Soldier, Beautiful Enemy	Diane Gaston
Winning the War Hero's Heart	Mary Nichols
Hostage Bride	Anne Herries

MEDICAL ROMANCE™

Tempted by Dr Daisy	Caroline Anderson
The Fiancée He Can't Forget	Caroline Anderson
A Cotswold Christmas Bride	Joanna Neil
All She Wants For Christmas	Annie Claydon

Mills & Boon® Large Print

October 2011

ROMANCE

Passion and the Prince	Penny Jordan
For Duty's Sake	Lucy Monroe
Alessandro's Prize	Helen Bianchin
Mr and Mischief	Kate Hewitt
Her Desert Prince	Rebecca Winters
The Boss's Surprise Son	Teresa Carpenter
Ordinary Girl in a Tiara	Jessica Hart
Tempted by Trouble	Liz Fielding

HISTORICAL

Secret Life of a Scandalous Debutante	Bronwyn Scott
One Illicit Night	Sophia James
The Governess and the Sheikh	Marguerite Kaye
Pirate's Daughter, Rebel Wife	June Francis

MEDICAL ROMANCE™

Taming Dr Tempest	Meredith Webber
The Doctor and the Debutante	Anne Fraser
The Honourable Maverick	Alison Roberts
The Unsung Hero	Alison Roberts
St Piran's: The Fireman and Nurse Loveday	Kate Hardy
From Brooding Boss to Adoring Dad	Dianne Drake